CHRISTY'S CHOICE

of Cutter Gap

CHRISTY'S CHOICE

Christy
of Cutter Gap

THE SERIES

Based on the novel Christy *by*

CATHERINE MARSHALL

EVERGREEN
— FARM —
an imprint of
GILEAD PUBLISHING

Christy's Choice: The Christy® of Cutter Gap series
Adapted by C. Archer
Copyright © 1995 by Marshall-LeSourd, LLC

EVERGREEN
— FARM —

Published by Evergreen Farm, an imprint of Gilead Publishing, LLC,
Wheaton, Illinois, USA.
www.gileadpublishing.com/evergreenfarm

ISBN: 978-1-68370-177-4 (printed softcover)
ISBN: 978-1-68370-178-1 (ebook)

Cover design by Larry Taylor
Cover illustrations © Larry Taylor. All rights reserved.
Interior design by Beth Shagene
Ebook production by Book Genesis, Inc.

Printed in the United States of America.

18 19 20 21 22 23 24 / 5 4 3 2 1

The Characters

Christy Rudd Huddleston, a nineteen-year-old girl

Christy's Students:
    Creed Allen, nine
    Bessie Coburn, twelve
    Sam Houston Holcombe, nine
    Ruby Mae Morrison, thirteen

David Grantland, the young minister

Ida Grantland, David's sister

Alice Henderson, a Quaker mission worker from Ardmore, Pennsylvania

Dr. Neil MacNeill, the physician of the Cove

Lety Coburn, mother of Christy's student, Bessie

Kyle Coburn, Bessie's father

Fairlight Spencer, a mountain woman

Granny Barclay, the midwife of the Cove

Mr. Huddleston, Christy's father

Mrs. Huddleston, Christy's mother

George Huddleston, Christy's brother

Lance Barclay, a young man from Asheville

Mr. Barclay, Lance's father

Mrs. Barclay, Lance's mother

Mabel Bentley, Melissa Bentley, Elizabeth Deerfield, and
Jeanette Grady, Christy's friends from Asheville

Thomas Wolfe, a boy from Asheville

One

Squeal! Squeeeeal!

Christy Huddleston was standing in front of her class writing on the blackboard when suddenly the hogs began squealing at the top of their lungs.

Squeeeeeal! Squeeeeeeal!

"What on earth?" Christy wondered aloud.

"Teacher, them ol' hogs is scared somethin' awful," Sam Houston Holcombe said.

"Must be a varmint got in with them," nine-year-old Creed Allen agreed. "Them's the sounds of hogs that are mighty afeared."

Squeeeeal! Squeeeeeeeal!

Christy put down her chalk. She sighed and rolled her eyes up to heaven. "Why me?" she whispered. She had to be the only teacher in the world who had hogs living under her classroom.

The hogs lived in the cool, dark mud beneath the school building, which also served as a church on Sundays. In rustic Cutter Gap, high up in the Great Smoky Mountains of

Tennessee, the mountain people were too poor to afford two separate buildings.

Since the building provided some shelter for the hogs, Christy had learned to accept them—even though sometimes their smell was quite unpleasant.

Squeeeal! Squeeeeeeeeeal!

Suddenly a loud banging came from underneath the floorboards. The hogs were squealing louder and louder. They were making so much noise that Christy knew she couldn't continue with her lessons.

She walked down the aisle toward the trapdoor that led down to the hogs. "I suppose we had better see what's going on," she said.

"Ma'am, you might best be careful," Creed warned. "Them hogs is acting downright fitified!"

"Well, I have to see—" Christy started to say.

Suddenly the trapdoor jumped upward with a bang. Christy took a step back.

With a second blow, the door flew open, and a huge hog came leaping up from below. In a panic, it scrabbled on the wooden floor, then ran right for Christy.

"Look out!" Sam Houston yelled.

Christy snatched up her skirts just in the nick of time. The hog went flying through her legs, leaving a smear of mud on Christy's stockings.

Squeeeal! The hog tore around the room, banging into everything in its path.

"It's after me!" thirteen-year-old Ruby Mae Morrison cried. She jumped up on a chair. "Keep away, you old hog!"

Then a second hog seemed to explode up from below. A third hog followed.

"Look out!" Christy yelled. "Everyone be careful!"

Now there were three crazy hogs racing madly around the classroom. Children jumped out of their way. Desks were overturned. Books went flying. Papers were blown every which way.

Sam Houston stuck his head down into the hole and said, "I reckon I know why them hogs is so scared, Miz Christy. There's a fox down in there with them."

"Someone grab these hogs!" Christy said. "They are destroying the classroom."

"Dumb old hogs," Sam Houston said. "Can't no little fox hurt them none."

Squeeeul! Again one of the hogs ran straight for Christy. She jumped aside. But when she jumped, she bumped into a second hog, which knocked her off balance.

"Look out, Teacher!" Creed Allen yelled.

Christy teetered on the edge of the opening in the floor. Down below, she could see the quizzical gaze of the little fox, looking up at her. She windmilled her arms, trying to keep her balance. But it was no use.

"Aaaaaah!" she cried.

Down she fell. Down through the hole in the floor. Down into the mud.

She landed with a plop. The fox took one look at her and ran.

When she looked up, Christy could see the faces of her students peering down at her.

Then, one by one, three more faces appeared. The first was David Grantland, the handsome young preacher who ran the mission.

He smiled. "Is this some new teaching method, Christy?" he asked.

The second face belonged to Miss Alice Henderson, the Quaker missionary who had founded the mission. She poked her head over the huddled students. Christy could tell she was trying very hard not to grin.

"Why, Miss Huddleston," said Miss Alice. "Whatever are you doing down there?"

The last face to appear belonged to Dr. Neil MacNeill. He didn't even try to hide his smile. Instead, he laughed outright.

"No, no, Christy," he said. "It's supposed to be you in the classroom and the hogs down below. Not the other way around."

"Very funny, all of you," Christy said through gritted teeth.

David stuck his hand down. "Come on, I'll help you up."

Christy tried to climb up out of the hole. But the sticky mud held on to her skirts and resisted her attempt to escape. She slipped and fell back again. One of her shoes was so stuck she had to unlace it to get free.

Finally, after several tries, she emerged back into her classroom. The three hogs had been shooed outside. But it was too late to save Christy's dress. Or her dignity. She was covered from head to toe with mud.

"You're not setting a very good example for the students," David said with a laugh as the others joined in.

"I'm glad you're all enjoying this," Christy said.

"Actually, we came to discuss a serious matter with you," Dr. MacNeill said. Then he wrinkled his nose. "But I think first you might want to see about a bath."

"I'll watch the class," David volunteered.

Christy left David in charge of the class and marched out of the schoolhouse to the mission. She was definitely not in a happy mood.

Miss Ida, David Grantland's older sister, stood in the doorway of the mission house. "Surely, Miss Huddleston, you don't intend to track all that mud into my clean parlor!" she exclaimed.

Christy just glared at her.

Miss Ida decided it might be best to step aside.

Twenty minutes later, Christy felt almost human again. She had taken a quick bath, using plenty of soap, and had put on a fresh skirt and blouse. She found Dr. MacNeill and Miss Alice in the parlor, waiting patiently for her.

Christy set down the basket she was carrying, filled with her muddy clothes. It was going to take hours to get them clean. They seemed to have picked up ten pounds of mud.

"Feeling better, Christy?" Miss Alice asked.

"Yes, Miss Alice, I am. I apologize if I seemed ungracious before."

"Ungracious?" Dr. MacNeill said. "You looked like you would have bitten the head off anyone who crossed your path."

"I believe Christy had reason enough to be snappish," Miss Alice said kindly. "Perhaps you had best tell her your news, Neil."

The doctor grew serious. He leaned forward in his chair. "It's Bessie Coburn," he said.

At the mention of Bessie, Christy's face clouded with concern. Bessie, who was thirteen, was Ruby Mae's best friend. The two of them were inseparable. Since Ruby Mae lived right in the mission house, Bessie was often there too. That is, until very recently, when she'd become ill.

"Is Bessie's condition worse?" Christy asked the doctor.

"Yes. I'm afraid it is," Dr. MacNeill said. "Much worse."

Two

"BESSIE IS IN INCREASING PAIN," DR. MACNEILL CONTIN-
ued, "and it will only get worse. I am certain now that we are
dealing with some sort of a cyst or abscess. I don't believe it's
life threatening—at least not yet. But it is very painful. It will
have to be removed."

"Surgery?" Christy asked. "Poor Bessie. She's just a child."

"Yes, we'll have to perform surgery. And it is more than
I can handle here in Cutter Gap. I need the facilities of a real
hospital. And I would dearly love to consult with Dr. Hugo
Mecklen. He is a surgeon who specializes in this area of
medicine."

"Whatever it takes to help Bessie," Christy said. "Only . . .
what about the money?"

"Naturally, I'll contribute my services free of charge," Dr.
MacNeill said. "And I believe Hugo will as well."

"But there are still the costs of the hospital itself, and of
medicines," Miss Alice said. "We all know that the mission
doesn't have much money. But I don't see how we can avoid
this expense. It will mean no more books or school supplies

for a while." Miss Alice smiled confidently. "But we have always managed."

Christy bit her lip. No books! Already the children were sharing books between two, and sometimes even three, students. But of course Bessie's health came first.

"I've already spoken to some friends on the railroad, and they've generously agreed to let Bessie and her companions travel for free," Miss Alice said.

"We'll be leaving as soon as we can get Bessie's parents to agree," Dr. MacNeill said. "Once that's arranged, we'll only have one problem."

"What problem?" Christy asked.

"It's not a very big problem," Miss Alice said, with a grin. "It's simply that we'll need someone to travel with Bessie. Her mother can't go. Not only is she expecting another baby soon, but she's needed to help plant the corn crop. Anyway, we thought perhaps you might wish to go."

"Me?"

"The hospital I'll be taking Bessie to is the one in Asheville," the doctor explained with a smile. "You could turn it into a visit home."

Home.

Christy glanced at the basket filled with her muddy clothes. Her mind traveled back to her home in Asheville. There in her room was a large oak wardrobe, a lovely armoire. Inside hung a dozen or more dresses. Clean dresses, clean blouses, clean everything.

Here in Cutter Gap, it seemed, nothing was ever truly clean. No matter how hard they all tried.

She pictured her tidy, well-decorated room. There were lace curtains on the windows and rugs on the floors.

Here at the mission, her room was almost a cell by comparison.

Most of all, she pictured her bed. Her big, fluffy, soft feather bed.

Had she ever been able to sleep as well here on her lumpy secondhand mattress?

"So will you go with the doctor and Bessie to Asheville?" Miss Alice asked.

"And me," David added as he strode into the middle of the room. "I'll be going too."

"I take it all's well at the schoolhouse?"

David grinned. "The children are on their way home, and the hogs are back where they belong. I just stopped by to see how Christy was doing."

"Well, she's no longer covered in mud, if that's what you mean." The doctor grinned, then added, "And I don't see any reason why we need you along on the trip, Reverend."

Christy exchanged a knowing glance with Miss Alice. The doctor and David were both "sweet" on Christy, as Ruby Mae liked to say. "The doctor and the preacher are like two hungry old coon dogs, circling around one bone," she'd told Christy once.

Christy wasn't sure she liked being compared to a bone. But she supposed there was some truth to what Ruby Mae said. In fact, David made no secret of his affections. He had even proposed marriage. Christy had turned down his offer, but with the understanding that she might reconsider at a later time. David was very special to her.

As for Neil MacNeill, well, he clearly didn't want her to marry David, but most of the time it was hard for Christy to know what was going on in his mind. Her feelings toward him were usually equal parts affection and annoyance.

"I'll be going to Asheville on mission business," David said. "I've been invited many times to visit some of the churches there and tell them about our work at the mission." He looked at Miss Alice. "I know we never ask for contributions, but if I were to go to Asheville and tell the people there about our work, and if they happened to want to help us . . ."

"We would never decline help," Miss Alice agreed. "As long as it's freely given, from the heart."

"I see," Dr. MacNeill said skeptically. "All of a sudden, just because Christy is going to Asheville, you are moved by an urgent need to visit your fellow preachers? Isn't that just a bit of a coincidence?"

"I have as much right to go to Asheville as—" David began.

Miss Alice interrupted him. "Gentlemen, gentlemen. Please. I don't believe Christy has even agreed to go."

"Oh, she'll go," said the doctor. "If I am not mistaken, she is already seeing visions in her head of clean sheets and cozy fires and meals that do not involve possum stew."

Christy started, jerked out of her daydream. It was very annoying, the way Neil could sometimes read her mind.

"I'll go to see my family," Christy said frostily. "And to help Bessie. She's the only thing that's really important here. Not because I'm thinking of those other things, Neil."

"There is still one problem," the doctor said. "As I mentioned, I haven't yet obtained permission from Kyle and Lety Coburn to perform the operation on Bessie."

"But why would they object?" Christy questioned in surprise.

The doctor shrugged. "I suppose it's a combination of things," he said. "Fear of losing their daughter. I've admitted to the Coburns that no operation is ever one hundred percent safe. And then, there's the usual problem: the Coburns are a very traditional clan. Kyle Coburn still believes in the old ways, the mountain cures."

"So Bessie might have to suffer?" Christy was outraged. She had tried to learn to respect the traditions of the mountain people, but to turn away from modern medicine at a time like this was simply foolish.

"Don't worry," David said. "I'm sure Kyle Coburn will come around in the end."

"Yes, I'm sure you're right, Reverend," the doctor said. Then, with a sly grin at Christy, he added, "You'll get your trip to the city yet, Christy."

"Let me make this clear, Neil," Christy said. "My only concern is for Bessie. I just want her to get better. The fact that the hospital happens to be in Asheville is unimportant." She stood up. "Now, if you'll excuse me, I have work to do."

She grabbed the basket of muddy, hog-smelling clothes. What she'd told the doctor was true—Bessie was all that really mattered to her. Still, she thought as she wrinkled her nose at the smell, it wouldn't really hurt to enjoy a few nights in her old room.

⊂#⊃

After she had cleaned the hog smell out of her dress, Christy decided to go visit Bessie and see how she was doing. Perhaps she would get an opportunity to talk some sense into Kyle Coburn.

"Can I come along?" Ruby Mae asked. "I ain't seen Bessie since yesterday."

"Sure, Ruby Mae. That is, if Miss Ida doesn't need you."

"No, Miz Christy. I tried to help her with her cooking, but she said I was just chitter-chattering so she couldn't hardly hear herself think. That's what she said."

Christy smiled. Ruby Mae did have a tendency to talk constantly, while Miss Ida preferred peace and quiet.

"All right, Ruby Mae, I'd be pleased if you'd come along with me."

It was late in the afternoon, but now that it was practically summer, the days lasted longer. Christy hoped to make it to the Coburn cabin and get back before it was dark, in plenty of time for dinner.

It was a pleasant walk. The day was warm, and wildflowers bloomed yellow and blue and pink in the grassy meadows.

Christy had long since accustomed herself to Ruby Mae's stream of chatter. She listened with one ear to Ruby Mae and with the other to the songs of the birds that were arriving back in the mountains after their winter escape to warmer southern climates.

They were close to the Coburn cabin when something Ruby Mae said seemed to jump out at her.

"What was that you just said, Ruby Mae?" Christy asked.

"I was just sayin' as how when we're in Asheville it would be fine if we could look into some of those shops where you get your citified clothing."

"When we are in Asheville?" Christy repeated.

"Yes, Miz Christy. Didn't you know? I'm a-goin' too."

"Who says you're going? Did Dr. MacNeill ask you to go along?"

Ruby Mae looked thoughtful. "I don't recollect rightly if it was the doctor. I just know I'm a-goin.'"

"Ruby Mae, I don't think—" Christy began.

Suddenly there came a low, sad moan, carried on the wind.

Christy pointed. "It's coming from the Coburn's cabin!"

"That's Bessie!" Ruby Mae cried.

"Ooooh, it hurts," the girl groaned. "Somebody help me, please!"

Three

CHRISTY RAN TOWARD THE CABIN, WITH RUBY MAE RIGHT behind her.

"Oooh, it hurts," the voice wailed.

Christy stumbled up the uneven wooden steps and burst through the door. Inside, Bessie lay on a simple cot. Her blond hair was matted and tangled. Strands of it were glued to her forehead by sweat.

"Bessie, what's wrong?" Christy cried.

Bessie's mother suddenly appeared in the doorway behind them. She had an armful of small branches and twigs. She ignored Christy and Bessie and ran to her daughter. "Is it bad again?" she asked.

"Yes, Ma, it hurts somethin' fierce."

Mrs. Coburn dropped the wood near the fireplace. Close by was a small, handmade cupboard. A table, three crude chairs, and the one cot were the only other furnishings. The cabin was orderly and clean enough, but still smelled of smoke and cooking odors. The only light filtered through a single window, which was covered with oiled paper instead of glass.

Mrs. Coburn went to the little cupboard and pulled out a bottle and a spoon.

"Here you go, sweetie," she said. She poured a spoonful from the bottle and gave it to Bessie.

Christy cleared her throat. She felt awkward, having just barged uninvited into the Coburns' cabin. "I'm sorry to come in uninvited, Mrs. Coburn," she said, "but we heard Bessie crying out for help."

"You're welcome here anytime, Miz Christy," Mrs. Coburn said wearily. "I was out gathering wood for the fire. The nights are still cold."

"Is that some kind of medicine in the bottle?" Ruby Mae asked. She eyed the bottle suspiciously. "Does it taste just awful, Bessie?"

"It do," Bessie acknowledged in a gasping voice. "Only it sort of dulls the hurtin' too. So I reckon I don't mind the taste."

"Doctor says she should take a bit, but only when the pain gets to be considerable," Mrs. Coburn explained. "He says it's laudanum, and it makes folk get a craving if'n they ain't careful."

Christy was shocked. Laudanum was a very powerful drug. Bessie must be in terrible pain for Dr. MacNeill to have prescribed it.

Christy pulled Mrs. Coburn aside. "Mrs. Coburn, has Dr. MacNeill told you that he wants to take Bessie to Asheville for an operation?" she asked in a low voice.

"Yes'm, he talked about that to me and Kyle." Mrs. Coburn bit her lip and looked worried. "Kyle, he don't take no stock in all this medicine of the doctor's. He says if'n it's the Lord's will to take Bessie, then there ain't nothing that folks can do, and it'd be a sin to try."

"But Mrs. Coburn, the Lord also gives us our intelligence, so that we can help ourselves."

She nodded. "That's what I told Kyle. Only he don't take easy to newfangled ideas and such. He says he reckons he'll stick to the old ways."

Christy felt her anger rising. It was difficult to keep it in check sometimes. The mountain people resisted even the things that would clearly help them.

"But your husband can't just let Bessie lie there in pain!" Christy argued.

The mountain woman raised a hand. "Don't you be a frettin', Miz Christy. That man can't stand no argufyin', so he went off to hunt up some meat to help Bessie get her strength back. Generally, if I keeps at him, he comes around."

"Are you saying you think he'll let Bessie go for the operation?"

"Well, I reckon as how there'll be a bit more argufyin' and thrashin' out, but yes'm, he'll end up by letting her go." She smiled at her daughter. "Leastways, he would if'n Bessie herself was to ask him. He's a stubborn old coot, but he does love his little girl." Her eyes darkened. "Unless he was to start to drinkin' tonight. He gets right ornery and stubborn as a mule when he's been at the jug."

Christy took a deep breath to steady her emotions. So Bessie could probably have the operation—but only if her father stayed sober.

Patience, Christy ordered herself. *Patience*. Miss Alice had warned her, ever so gently, of course, that too much pushing and prodding would just create greater resistance. The mountain people had lived alone, without help from the world outside, for many, many years. It was only natural that they were suspicious of outsiders and set in their own ways.

Unfortunately, their own ways included bootleg liquor and ignorant superstitions.

"Dr. MacNeill has asked if I will go along to Asheville with him," Christy said. "And Reverend Grantland may be coming too."

"I'd be much obliged to you," Mrs. Coburn said. "It's fittin' that a woman would take care of my Bessie. It pains me mightily 'cause I cain't be going with Bessie myself. But our new baby will be comin' most any time now. Besides, plantin' season came late this year, and we have to get our corn in."

"Of course," Christy said. She knew that a family that didn't plant its crops in spring would starve in winter. Life in the mountains was harsh and unforgiving.

"Don't you worry none, Mrs. Coburn," Ruby Mae said. "Me and Miz Christy will see to Bessie."

"Are you going, too, Ruby Mae?" Bessie cried.

"Sure I am," Ruby Mae said.

"No, she's not," Christy said at the same instant.

"But I got to go, Miz Christy," Ruby Mae pleaded. "Who's Bessie gonna talk to?"

"Who am I gonna talk to, Miz Christy?" Bessie echoed.

"What do you mean, who's she going to talk to?" Christy said. "Why, to me, of course. And to the doctor and Rev. Grantland."

Bessie and Ruby Mae exchanged a look.

"Miz Christy, it ain't the same," Ruby Mae pointed out. "You bein' a teacher and all."

"I don't reckon I could even go all the way to Asheville less'n I had Ruby Mae to keep company with," Bessie agreed solemnly. "I don't even reckon I could ask my pa to let me go, unless . . ." Bessie gave Christy a sideways look.

Christy almost laughed. Bessie was blackmailing her! She was threatening not to have the operation unless Ruby Mae could go too. The laudanum had obviously relieved Bessie's pain enough to allow her to instantly fall in with Ruby Mae's plan.

"Bessie would be all alone in the big city with not a single friend," Ruby Mae added in a pleading voice.

"Powerful lonely is what I'd be," Bessie agreed. "I don't reckon a person can mend properly if they's all lonely and such."

"You hear that, Miz Christy?" Ruby Mae wailed. "Bessie could just up and die if'n I ain't with her."

Christy rolled her eyes. "I have the distinct feeling," she said with a sigh, "that I'm outnumbered."

⊂#⊃

That night as she lay in bed, Christy couldn't fall asleep. The wind had picked up as night fell, and now it whistled through every chink in the mission house. A loose board rattled and banged.

Rain began to fall. On the tin roof, it made a sound like gravel being thrown against a drum. She knew that in a few seconds, if the rain kept up, it would find its way through the roof and begin leaking from the ceiling.

She thought of the Coburns' cabin, so much rougher and cruder even than the mission house. Surely there, the wind was even more of a problem. Surely there, and in all the simple cabins of the poor mountain folk, the rain poured from a dozen leaks.

Christy knew she should be grateful for all she had. But at the same time she kept recalling her room in her parents' house back in Asheville. So quiet, even in the midst of a spring storm. So warm. So clean. The bed so soft.

She heard the sound of water. Drip . . . *drip* . . . *drip*. With a sigh, she threw back her covers and padded on bare feet across the cold wooden floor.

"Oww!" A nail had worked its way up from the planks. She hobbled over to her dresser and grabbed the pot she kept handy, then limped over to the corner, where the rain was now dripping in a steady stream. She stuck the pot under the drip.

The noise it made was like fingernails on a chalkboard.

"I'm far too awake now to fall asleep," she muttered.

She struck a match and lit a smoky oil lamp. Then she pulled her diary out of her nightstand and opened it.

June 7, 1912

It's been five months since I came to the Cutter Gap mission to teach school. Today I learned that I will be returning to Asheville for a visit. It will only be for a few days. Dr. MacNeill says they will do Bessie Coburn's operation the day after we arrive there. Then, if all goes well (and I pray it will), we will spend a few days there while Bessie recovers before returning.

It will be good to see Mother and Father and George, if he isn't away at school. I have so much to tell them. We've written each other every week, but it's impossible to tell everything in a letter. There's so much to catch up on. I wonder what has been happening in Asheville. I wonder what my old friends have been up to. And I know they are all curious about me.

And yet, in some ways, this trip scares me. Just a little.

I've grown accustomed to life in the Cove. I've grown used to the hostility of so many of the mountain people because it has been balanced by the affection of so many others who have become my friends. And I've grown used to the simple, everyday hardships because I know that for most of the people here life is much harder than what I have experienced.

I suppose I have even grown accustomed to the fact that a little girl's life might be held hostage to superstition and suspicion and bootleg whiskey. Although it makes me angry beyond words.

Still, as I think of visiting my home again, all the old memories come rushing back . . .

What will it be like to be clean again? Clean, all of the time!

What will it be like to speak with people who can talk of world events and art and poetry? Most of the mountain people say little, and then only of the necessary things: of crops and hunting and mending broken plows. What will it be like to once again talk of Paris fashions and New York literature?

Will I seem backward and rustic to all my old friends? And what will they make of Ruby Mae or David or Neil?

I should be looking forward to this trip. And yet it makes me uneasy. It makes me think of all I have given up to be here.

When I left Asheville, my head was full of romantic notions. I knew nothing about blood feuds and moonshine;

I understood nothing about the ignorance and fear that still live in these mountains. And I never thought about money—about whether this mission could even be kept alive.

Many of my romantic notions have been lost. I love my students, and I am devoted to the mission. But, knowing all the harsh realities, will I be able to leave my home and my family a second time? If I return to Asheville now, will I still have the devotion to come back to Cutter Gap?

Four

"Miz Christy, Miz Christy," Ruby Mae yelled. "Where are you, Miz Christy?"

"I'm right here, Ruby Mae," Christy said. It was Saturday morning, and Christy was walking toward the school with her arms full of flowers in every color of the rainbow. Fairlight Spencer was with her. "I just got back. What's the matter?"

"Howdy, Miz Spencer," Ruby Mae said. "What are all them flowers for?"

Fairlight was Christy's closest friend among the mountain people. Five of her children, including John and Zady, were in Christy's class. Fairlight was a simple woman, only now learning to read. But she had the bearing of a princess, and Christy admired her sense of wonder about life, as well as her common sense and decency.

"They're for the altar, for services tomorrow," Fairlight explained. "Aren't they lovely, Ruby Mae?"

"Yes'm, I 'spect they'll give me something to admire in church when I start to fall asleep during the sermon."

Fairlight and Christy exchanged an amused look.

Fortunately, David was not around to hear Ruby Mae's opinion of his sermons.

"I got to talk to you, quick-like, Miz Christy," Ruby Mae said, tugging on Christy's sleeve. "It's Bessie's pa. He got back all liquored up, and he and Mrs. Coburn, they got to argufyin' fit to wake the dead. And now he's got it all stuck in his head that Bessie can't be going to Asheville or having no operation, neither!"

Christy thought for a moment. She wished Miss Alice were there. But Miss Alice rode out regularly to check on the health needs of people in several small mountain communities, and she was away for the day. "Ruby Mae, go and saddle up Prince for me. I'm going for the doctor."

"Yes'm," Ruby Mae said. "Only how am I gonna keep up if you're on a horse?"

"I'm going alone. Just for once, don't argue, Ruby Mae."

"I'll take care of the flowers," Fairlight said. She put her hand on Christy's arm. "You be careful. Kyle Coburn is a decent man when he's sober. But if he's been at that jug, don't you be messin' with him."

⊂#⊃

Dr. MacNeill was on the roof of his house, nailing new wooden shingles. He watched Christy riding up, threading the twisting trails, then galloping across the meadow. He had a pretty good idea why she was coming. News traveled with amazing speed in the Cove. Sometimes he thought they would never need telephones in these hills, the way they could pass along gossip.

He took a moment to enjoy the sight before him: the mountains looming all around; the nearby brook that bubbled and leapt with new-melted snow; and the rather beautiful sight of Christy, her hair flying free in the wind as she galloped toward him on the mission's big black horse.

He climbed down from the roof and went inside for a shirt and his medical bag. When he came back out, Christy was just reining Prince to a halt.

"Well, good morning, Christy," he said.

"Doctor," she said, a little breathlessly. "It's Bessie. Her father—"

"Yes, I know all about it."

"You do?"

"Yep. In fact, I was just on my way to see Granny Barclay. I thought she might offer me her professional opinion on the case."

Neil paused, enjoying the look of confusion on Christy's face. "Prince is tired, by the look of him," he said. "We'll go on foot."

"But why on earth would we go to Granny Barclay?" Christy protested.

"Before I got here, Granny Barclay was the closest thing to a doctor this cove had seen. Would you prefer that I went stomping up to the Coburns' cabin to lecture Kyle Coburn on what he should do?" Neil asked. "That would just get his pride up, and then there would be no moving him."

"Well, we certainly have to do something."

"Yes. But not always the most direct thing," Neil said. "You can come along, if you wish."

With that, he set out at a brisk pace. He was not at all surprised that Christy followed him.

It was a mile to Granny Barclay's simple cabin. The old woman sat on her porch on a rocking chair made of bent sticks wrapped with vines. Her face was deeply wrinkled. Most of her teeth were gone. But her green eyes still shone, bright, attentive, and shrewd. She showed no surprise at seeing Neil and Christy.

"Morning, Granny," Neil said. "May we have a word with you?"

"I'd be right proud to have you sit a spell with an old woman," Granny said.

"I find I have a little problem of a medical nature," Neil said. "It's Bessie Coburn. I was wondering if you might be so kind as to come with me to take a look at her."

Neil could see the shocked look on Christy's face.

"I reckon I could," Granny said. "I could do with a stretch."

Without another word, Granny set off in the direction of the Coburn cabin.

"Doctor, it must be two miles from here to the Coburn place, most of it either straight up or straight down," Christy whispered in Neil's ear as they followed the old woman. "Granny is eighty years old! She can't possibly walk that far."

"I think you may be mistaken about that, Christy," Neil replied. "First of all, she's closer to ninety. Now, let's hurry, or we won't be able to catch up with her."

Granny Barclay set a pace that soon had Christy and Neil panting and sweating. A dozen yards from the Coburns' cabin, Granny finally stopped. She made a show of rubbing her shoulder. "I guess these old bones o' mine ain't got quite the life they used to. I don't 'spec I could walk more'n another two, three hours at this pace."

Christy wiped the sweat from her brow and groaned. "Granny isn't quite as frail as she looks," Neil said.

Christy laughed ruefully. "So I've noticed."

Granny Barclay cackled happily.

Inside the Coburn cabin, they found Bessie still in her bed. Lety Coburn was wiping her brow. Kyle Coburn sat in a corner, looking angry and sullen.

Neil took a quick look around. There was no liquor jug in evidence. And Kyle appeared to be sober, if a bit hung over.

"Kyle, Lety," Neil said, "I've asked Granny Barclay if she would be so kind as to consult with me on Bessie's case."

Kyle stared hard. "You askin' for Granny's help?" he demanded suspiciously. "I was a-fixin' to ask Granny to come over myself. She midwifed at Bessie's birth. And she helped me that time I had the fever."

"Let me see the child," Granny said, bustling over to Bessie's bedside.

"I didn't think you city folk put no stock in Granny's medicine," Kyle said doubtfully.

"Granny has delivered more babies than I've ever seen," Neil said honestly. "And she has a great store of wisdom."

Kyle nodded. "And Granny don't go around cuttin' folks open, neither. No good comes of cuttin' a body open. That just stands to reason."

"Yes," Neil agreed, "it is dangerous to perform surgery."

Kyle sat forward suddenly. "So you admit right out it be dangerous! My little girl could die."

This was the real reason Kyle had resisted the surgery, Neil knew. He was just worried about his daughter.

Neil looked Kyle straight in the eye. "Yes, she could die," he said gently. "There could be complications."

Granny patted Bessie on the head and stood. "There's a lump inside that girl where don't no lump belong," she announced. "That's what's causing the pain and the fever."

"Cain't you do nothin' to make it go away?" Kyle pleaded.

"I can help ease the pain, but only a little," Granny said. "I can give her some bark tea and some other potions that will take the edge off'n the hurt. But that won't help for long. The pain will go right on getting worse till it overcomes all medicine."

Kyle looked shattered. "There ain't nothing you can do, Granny?"

"There's something I can do," Neil said. "I can take her to Asheville, to a real hospital. And I can get the best man in the area to help me do the operation."

"Kyle, you got to let them try," Lety urged, fighting back tears.

Kyle looked tortured. "I have to send my little girl off to some city and not even know whether she's livin' or dyin'? What am I supposed to do? I can't just sit here a-doin' nothing."

"Kyle, you have to trust to modern medical science," Neil said. But the man looked unmoved.

"There is something you can do," Christy said, speaking for the first time. "You can pray that God will guide Dr. Mac-Neill's hand and keep Bessie well."

When Neil and Christy went back outside several minutes later, they had received Kyle's permission to do the operation. Granny stayed behind to brew up her pain-fightin' bark tea.

"That was very clever of you, Doctor," Christy said. "You knew Kyle was holding out hope that Granny could save Bessie from having to undergo surgery. So you brought Granny over."

"It's something you should learn, Christy. The head-on approach isn't always the best. I could have argued myself blue, but by asking Granny's opinion, I made Kyle realize he had no choice."

"It seemed to me that Mr. Coburn was still doubtful about the operation, even then," Christy said. "He needed to feel he could be involved in some way."

"You mean the thing about praying?" Neil nodded. "Yes, I suppose that did make him feel as if he were doing something to help his daughter."

"But you don't believe it."

"What? That God is guiding my hands when I'm performing surgery? No. I believe in medicine and science. When my knowledge and skill are sufficient, I am successful."

"I see," Christy said, arms crossed over her chest. "So your advice to Mr. Coburn would be to believe in Almighty Dr. MacNeill rather than Almighty God?"

Neil had to laugh. "Well, when you put it that way, I suppose it does sound just a wee bit egotistical."

Christy shook her head, giving him a grudging smile. "Yes," she agreed, "just a wee bit."

Five

THE TRAIN WHISTLE BLEW SHRILLY. IT WAS SO LOUD THAT
even though she was sitting in the next-to-last car, Christy
covered her ears. It was an exciting sound, full of promises
of adventure. But the sound was also full of memories. It had
been this very train—Old Buncombe, they called it—that had
first carried Christy away from home last January.

It was Monday morning. Yesterday, after church, they had
carried Bessie to El Pano, the nearest town on the railroad
line. Miss Alice had arranged for them to stay overnight with
a friend. Bessie had rested fairly well last night. Then, early
this morning, they had caught the train for Asheville.

Christy was sitting beside David. Behind them, Bessie
lay across both seats, with the doctor nearby across the aisle.
Bessie looked very pale and weak, but the combination of the
doctor's medicine and Granny Barclay's tea seemed to have
her pain under control.

Ruby Mae seemed unable to sit anywhere for more than
two seconds.

"Are we going yet?" she asked excitedly, leaning over Christy and David to look out the window.

The train lurched forward and sent Ruby Mae sprawling over Christy's lap.

"Now we're going," Christy said with a laugh.

"Sorry, Miz Christy," Ruby Mae said breathlessly, taking a seat behind Bessie. "I ain't been on no train afore. It's got me as jittery as a bug on a hot skillet."

The train began to pick up speed and pull away from the little station house at El Pano.

"Lordamercy!" Ruby Mae said. "We're practically flying! Look at how the trees just shoot right past till they's nothin' but a blur."

"I'd guess we're going at least twenty miles per hour now," David said. "We'll get up close to forty on the flatter stretches of track."

"It don't seem possible," Ruby Mae said. "Aren't you excited, Bessie? Ain't this just the best thing ever?"

Bessie managed a tired smile. "It is a wonder," she agreed.

"You let me know if the pain gets worse," Dr. MacNeill told her.

Ruby Mae chattered on, remarking on every new twist and turn in the railroad track. And there were plenty of twists and turns. Sometimes it was impossible to see any ground outside the window, because the track ran right along the edge of sheer drops that plunged down hundreds of feet. Here and there Christy caught sight of tumbledown shacks stuck back in the trees. They were gray and shabby, just like the homes of most of her students. No running water, no telephones, no indoor plumbing, none of the luxuries that people in the cities took for granted. Sometimes it seemed as if these small cabins had been marooned there, trapped by the sheer walls of the mountains and unable to escape.

The train wound through tunnels and across narrow bridges over the swollen river below. At times it climbed slowly, straining against the force of gravity drawing it downward. But with each turn, the mountains opened a bit wider. The flat stretches grew longer. The curves grew less extreme.

They had only been traveling for seven hours, but it seemed to Christy that Cutter Gap was a million miles behind them.

And then she saw it: Asheville.

It, too, lay nestled in the valleys between mountains. But these mountains were small and tame. Here, the houses were white-painted clapboard or dark brick. There were proper chimneys poking through steep shingled roofs. Streets were paved in most areas, with curbs and shade trees in neat lines. Everywhere she looked, Christy saw telephone wires strung on tall poles.

As the train slowed to enter town, it ran parallel to a road. A beautiful dark-blue Deusenberg motorcar, driven by a white-gloved chauffeur, kept pace for a while.

"Look at that!" Ruby Mae exclaimed. "That's one of them automobiles! My, don't it look fine?"

"Yes, it's probably heading for the Biltmore estate," Christy said. The Biltmore estate, which belonged to the famous Vanderbilt family, was more of a palace than a home. It rivaled anything ever created by French kings or English lords.

"Do you know the Vanderbilts?" Dr. MacNeill asked.

Christy blushed. "Of course not. I've never met Mr. Vanderbilt. Although I have seen him in Pack Square on occasion.

I don't suppose he will be in town at this time of the year. The high season doesn't begin until summer."

"Ah, yes. When all the idle rich who live off the labor of others escape from sweltering New York and steamy Richmond and stuffy Washington, D.C.," Dr. MacNeill said gruffly. "They come to the mountains to breathe fresh air for three months."

Somehow, Christy got the impression the doctor did not entirely approve of Asheville's wealthier residents.

She noticed him looking critically at a frayed patch on his jacket. Was he actually feeling unsure of himself? Was he self-conscious about looking rustic? It didn't seem possible that Neil MacNeill could ever feel uncertain about anything.

She glanced over at David. He was looking out of the window. His gaze seemed to be drawn to each church steeple that came into view. His face looked troubled and a little wistful.

"That's the church I was baptized in," Christy said, pointing to a particular stone steeple. "I used to sing in the choir. Badly, I'm afraid. That's the church where you've been invited to speak."

"A church that size must have quite a congregation," David said thoughtfully.

Christy noticed that even Ruby Mae had fallen silent. She, too, was staring out of the window, looking just a little intimidated.

"Are you excited to be here at last?" Christy asked her.

"Folks has all got so much here," she answered. "Automobiles and fine houses and such. I seen some of the women as we passed by. They was all dressed fit for a wedding or a funeral. I don't s'pose these fine ladies would even stoop to speak to someone who looked like me."

"Ruby Mae, that's not true," Christy said earnestly. "This is where I come from. And have I ever been haughty to you?"

"No, Miz Christy," Ruby Mae said. She smiled in relief. "I 'spec you're right. Folks is just folks, no matter how they look on the outside."

"I'm sure you'll have a good time in Asheville, Ruby Mae," Christy assured her. Still, she couldn't help recalling the way some residents had behaved cruelly toward mountain people visiting the city. They called them hillbillies or hicks, among other names.

"I'll tell you what, Ruby Mae," Christy said. "I have more dresses than I could ever need. We'll find something that will fit you just fine, if you like. And we'll get something nice for Bessie too. Pretty soon she'll be back on her feet, and we'll all be having a wonderful time together."

But as she smiled reassuringly at her friends, all she saw in their faces was worry.

⌒

They were met at the station by Christy's parents.

"Christy!" they cried in unison.

"Father! Mother!" Christy ran to their open arms. "You haven't changed, either of you," she said when at last they released her.

"Of course not," Mr. Huddleston said. "It's been less than six months. What did you expect? To find me with a white beard down to the ground?"

"It seems as if so much time has passed," Christy said. She turned to her friends. David and Neil were busy helping Bessie from the train onto a stretcher.

Christy felt a pang of guilt. She should have helped Bessie first before rushing to see her parents.

"This is one of my students, Ruby Mae Morrison," Christy said.

"Ruby Mae!" Mrs. Huddleston practically yelled in excitement. "It's Ruby Mae!"

Ruby Mae looked startled.

"You must understand, Ruby Mae," Mr. Huddleston explained, "Christy writes us letters full of all the events in Cutter Gap. She always mentions you in those letters. We feel as if we know all about you."

"You write about me in letters?" Ruby Mae asked Christy.

"I only tell people the good parts," Christy teased.

"And that must be Dr. MacNeill and David Grantland," Mrs. Huddleston said.

The two men carried Bessie on a stretcher toward a waiting ambulance for the ride to the hospital. The doctor helped make her comfortable inside while David joined Christy and the others.

"Very pleased to meet you both," David said, extending his hand.

"Reverend, we'll be going now, if you're coming," Dr. MacNeill called out. "Oh, and pleased to make your acquaintance, Mr. and Mrs. Huddleston. I must apologize for hurrying off, but—"

"We understand perfectly," Mr. Huddleston said quickly. "The young lady's health is infinitely more important than introductions. Please, we'll all meet later at the house."

"I should go with them," Christy said.

"Are you coming, Reverend?" the doctor asked again.

"I'll be right there," David called.

"I'm coming too," Christy said.

"I'm sure the two men can manage quite well," Mrs. Huddleston said. She put a hand on Christy's arm. "Why don't you and Ruby Mae come with us? Your father is dying to show you his new toy."

"What new toy?"

Christy's father grinned. "I bought one of Mr. Ford's Model Ts."

"You bought a new automobile?" Christy cried in surprise.

"I did indeed," Mr. Huddleston said, beaming.

"Miz Christy! Miz Christy! I ain't never rode in an automobile," Ruby Mae said excitedly. "Lordamercy! A train and an automobile, all in the same day. Won't the others back in the Cove just curl up and die o' green envy when I tell them?"

"Go ahead, Christy," Dr. MacNeill said. "Ruby Mae will never forgive you if she doesn't get her Model T ride. And there's no room in the ambulance anyway. It'll be cramped as it is. You can stop by and visit Bessie later."

As Neil, David, and Bessie pulled away in the ambulance, Christy felt a strange sensation. It seemed wrong, somehow, to let them go without her. Still, it was certainly true that she wasn't needed at the hospital. And she and Ruby Mae would both be there for the operation.

Just the same, Christy felt she'd made a mistake, as if she'd failed some test for which she was unprepared.

"Come along, dear," her father said, reaching for her arm. "Let's take you home."

Six

THE RIDE IN THE MODEL T WAS EXCITING, ESPECIALLY since Christy's father was bursting with pride in the new machine. They took the "scenic route," as Mr. Huddleston called it. It took twice as long to get home as it would have if they had simply walked. He drove all over town showing Ruby Mae the sights. Ruby Mae never seemed to run out of energy, but Christy soon tired. They'd been up since long before sunrise, and it was now late in the afternoon.

Finally, they arrived at Christy's home. To her surprise, it felt familiar, yet somehow alien. It was as if she had never left, and yet, at the very same time, as if she'd been gone forever.

When she went inside and climbed the stairs, Christy found her room completely unchanged. It was just the way she had left it. There stood the desk where she had done her school lessons when she was younger. It sat nestled against the window so she could look out over the street and watch the horse wagons and automobiles pass by.

There was her armoire, door open to reveal the dresses,

skirts, and bright blouses she hadn't been able to take with her to Cutter Gap. On the shelves above sat hat boxes.

And there stood her oak vanity with the oval mirror. The brushes and combs she had chosen not to take with her were still neatly laid out on a starched lace doily.

Christy sat down on the velvet stool and looked at her image in the mirror. It was startling. There weren't any major changes in her reflection, just so many small ones. Her hair had not been properly cut in some time, and it was somewhat dull and lifeless. When she had lived here at home, she had brushed it a hundred strokes each night. But that habit was hard to keep up at the mission, where she often simply collapsed in exhaustion at the end of a trying day.

Her face was windburned and red from the sun. And her hands were no longer as soft as they had been. She often did her own laundry now at the mission with harsh lye soap.

"Miz Christy?"

Christy saw Ruby Mae appear in the mirror behind her. She turned around. Ruby Mae looked awestruck, like someone entering a great cathedral.

"Come in, Ruby Mae," Christy said.

"Was this your room?"

"Yes, this is my room."

Ruby Mae wandered around slowly. She touched the books on their shelves. She went to the armoire and just stared, dumbfounded.

"Are all these yours?" she whispered.

"Yes, they are," Christy said. "I know it seems like an awful lot of things . . ."

But Ruby Mae wasn't listening. She went to the bed and reverently stroked the soft down comforter.

Suddenly Christy felt terribly uncomfortable. Ruby Mae lived at the mission now, but before that she had lived in a cabin as rough and simple as any in the Cove. All her life she had seen nothing but simple, crude furniture, and homespun hand-me-down clothing. Most of the children in the Cove didn't even wear shoes. Most didn't own a pair of shoes.

"Come on, let's go back downstairs," Christy said brightly. "Mother will have tea ready for us."

"I ain't never seen nothin' near to this," Ruby Mae said, sweeping her arm around the room. "This is like some palace where those far-off kings of old lived, like you told us about at school."

"It's certainly not a palace," Christy said. "It's no grander than the other houses on this street."

Ruby Mae shook her head. "Miz Christy, if you collected every fine thing in all the Cove and put it all together, you couldn't touch this one room."

Christy stood up suddenly. Ruby Mae was starting to annoy her now, making her feel guilty.

"There's only one thing I plumb don't understand," Ruby Mae said.

"What's that?"

"With all this . . . how come you ever leaved?"

The question surprised Christy. She took Ruby Mae's hand and pulled her toward the door. "Let's go downstairs and have that tea, shall we?" she said quickly.

⌒

Ruby Mae followed Miz Christy down the stairs. Even the stairs were amazing! There were framed pictures on the walls all the way down. And the stairs were actually carpeted. Rugs on the stairs. Who'd ever heard of such a thing?

"Did you find everything as you left it, Christy?" Mr. Huddleston asked.

"Just as if I'd never left," Miz Christy said.

"It was the purtiest room I ever did see," Ruby Mae said. "For sure, I ain't never seen the like."

"I'm glad you liked it," Mrs. Huddleston said. "We've fixed up the guest room for you. I hope you'll find it pleasant as well."

"This whole house is like goin' to heaven, only I ain't dead and there ain't no angels," Ruby Mae exclaimed.

Mr. Huddleston laughed loudly. Ruby Mae grinned, but then it occurred to her that maybe Mr. Huddleston was laughing at her. No, that wasn't likely, on second thought. He seemed like a very fine man.

"Will you take some tea, my dear?" Mrs. Huddleston asked. She held the teapot poised over a tiny cup.

"Yes'm," Ruby Mae said nervously.

"Milk, sugar?"

"No, ma'am, tea. Like you said."

"She means would you like your tea with milk, or with sugar, or maybe both," Miz Christy explained.

Ruby Mae swallowed hard. It was like one of Miz Christy's tests at school—there had to be a right answer, and there had to be a wrong answer. "I reckon I'll have whatever y'all have," she said warily.

"That would be sweet," Mrs. Huddleston said. "Christy has always had such a sweet tooth. It's amazing she's managed to keep her figure."

"Yes, ma'am," Ruby Mae said. "Only she don't eat much

most of the time. I reckon that's on account of the preacher and the doctor."

"Ruby Mae, I don't think—" Miz Christy said suddenly.

"Both of them are sparkin' to Miz Christy somethin' amazing, so it wouldn't do for her to be gettin' all fat and puffed up."

The pink blush that spread up Miz Christy's neck didn't surprise Ruby Mae. Her teacher always blushed whenever anyone talked about the way the preacher and the doctor both hankered for her.

Mrs. Huddleston just laughed and sent Ruby Mae a wink. But Mr. Huddleston looked a little troubled. He smiled, all right, but Ruby Mae could tell it wasn't a real smile.

Just then, there came a knock at the front door.

"I'll get it for you," Ruby Mae said. She opened the front door to reveal the preacher and Dr. MacNeill.

"Well, howdy," she said. Then, in a low whisper, she added, "Reckon you both better wipe your boots off real good. This is a mighty fine home."

The two men glanced at each other. If Ruby Mae hadn't known better, she'd have sworn they looked as nervous as she was feeling. They each carefully wiped their feet on the mat before entering.

Miz Christy jumped up. "Mother, Father, this, of course, is David Grantland, whom you met at the station. And this is Dr. Neil MacNeill."

"Pleased to formally make your acquaintance," the doctor said, shaking Mr. Huddleston's hand. "I'm sorry we had to run off at the station."

"We understand, Doctor," Mr. Huddleston said. "How is your patient doing?"

"She ain't a-hurtin' too much, is she?" Ruby Mae questioned anxiously.

"Not to worry, Ruby Mae. Bessie made the trip rather well. She was sleeping when we left the hospital," Dr. MacNeill said. "We'll be able to perform the operation first thing tomorrow morning."

"Did she ask where I was?" Miz Christy asked.

"Bessie understood that you were with your parents," he said. "I reassured her that you and Ruby Mae would be with her tomorrow."

"Would you gentlemen join us for some tea?" Mrs. Huddleston said.

"Perhaps they would like to go straight upstairs and check out their room," Mr. Huddleston said.

The preacher looked surprised. "Mr. Huddleston, we've made arrangements to stay at a boarding house."

"Nonsense," Mrs. Huddleston said. "Christy's brother, George, is away at boarding school, and his room is sitting empty. You must stay here with us."

"If they've already made arrangements, perhaps they'd rather . . ." Mr. Huddleston began to say.

Mrs. Huddleston cut him off. "They'll stay with us. And I'm sure they would both love a cup of tea before they go up to see the room. And they will of course be joining us this evening for the soiree."

"What soiree?" Miz Christy asked.

Swar-ray. Ruby Mae wondered that was. It sounded awful fancy, but she was afraid to ask outright. She'd talk to Miz Christy about it later, she decided.

"Why, the Barclays are having a few friends over, Christy," Mrs. Huddleston said. "It's in honor of your homecoming. I believe Lance will be there too. Lance is home from college for a while."

Ruby Mae saw her teacher jerk in surprise at the mention of the name Lance. At the same time, she saw the doctor raise his eyebrows and the preacher narrow his eyes. The two of them looked mighty curious.

"Lance Barclay?" Mr. Huddleston sent a doubtful look to his wife. "Maybe Christy would rather just have a quiet evening at home with her parents, whom she hasn't seen in months."

"We've already told the Barclays we would come," Mrs. Huddleston replied.

Ruby Mae hid a smile behind her hand. It was pretty clear to see that Mrs. Huddleston was pleased to have her daughter surrounded by courters, including this Lance fellow, whoever he was. She was just like any matchmaking mother back in the Cove.

And it was just as plain that Mr. Huddleston wanted no part of the preacher or the doctor or the fellow named Lance. Just the same as any nervous father back in the Cove.

Her first instinct had been right, Ruby Mae realized. Folks were just folks, even if they lived in fine houses.

"You will come, won't you, gentlemen?" Mrs. Huddleston asked. "I'm sure you'd both enjoy getting to know all of Christy's old friends. Especially Lance. He's such a pleasant young man."

The doctor and the preacher looked at each other suspiciously. Then they each looked at Miz Christy even more suspiciously.

"I'd be happy to go," the reverend said tersely.

"Oh, yes, we'll definitely be there," the doctor said with a twinkle in his eyes.

Ruby Mae couldn't help grinning to herself. This visit was getting more interesting by the minute.

Seven

"My, don't we all look so fine?" Ruby Mae said that evening. "If Bessie could just see me in this dress! Wouldn't she be green with envy?"

Christy and her mother had done some quick alterations on one of Christy's dresses. The dress was silk and lace and came with a small matching clutch purse and shoes with heels. Christy watched nervously as Ruby Mae balanced in the painfully tight shoes. They were planning to walk the two blocks to the Barclay home.

"I feel like a regular princess," Ruby Mae said. "Like out of a book."

"Are you sure your feet are all right?" Christy asked.

"Oh, yes, Miz Christy. It just takes some getting used to. It's kind of like the way you have to walk real careful and sort of on your toes when you cross the creek on the old log bridge."

"Silly, impractical things women's shoes are!" Dr. Mac-Neill chuckled.

The evening air was warm and scented with flowers. As

they neared the Barclay home, Christy noticed beautifully clothed passengers climbing out of expensive automobiles. The Barclays weren't as rich as the Vanderbilts, but they were well to do. Their house was larger than the Huddleston home. It had its own carriage house with servants' quarters above it.

There were lanterns strung in the trimmed bushes and trees in front of the house. Through the windows, Christy could see the glint of silver and crystal. At the door, a servant assisted arriving guests.

It wasn't nearly as elegant as the parties that went on at the big estates among the truly wealthy class. But to Christy's eyes, used to the subtler beauties of Cutter Gap, it seemed unbelievably bright and colorful and wondrous.

Inside the house, they were swept along to the large parlor. Most of the furniture had been removed to clear a large area for people to wander about and talk while munching delicate morsels of food. Later, Christy knew, there would be dancing on the gleaming wooden floor. In one corner, a string quartet played music by Beethoven.

Mrs. Barclay swept toward them. She was a somewhat heavy woman, with iron-gray hair and eyes to match. "Good evening, good evening! I'm so glad you were able to come on such short notice."

"Mrs. Barclay," Christy said, taking the woman's hand, "allow me to introduce my friends, the Reverend David Grantland, Dr. Neil MacNeill, and one of my students, Ruby Mae Morrison."

"Charmed," Mrs. Barclay said.

"Thanks for having us." The doctor smiled stiffly.

"There's a Barclay family in Cutter Gap," David said. "Are you perhaps related?"

Mrs. Barclay's eyes narrowed. "I am quite certain that I would never be related to anyone from . . . where is it? Carter Gap?"

"Cutter Gap," Dr. MacNeill corrected.

"Yes, of course. That's the quaint little hamlet in the hills where Christy teaches the unfortunate illiterates. Christy, your mother tells me what you write in your letters. It moves me to tears to think of you up there among moonshiners with their blood feuds. No offense meant," she added. "The mountaineers don't know any better, I suppose."

Christy felt a stab of embarrassment. She glanced at Ruby Mae, who just looked confused. Neil and David looked downright annoyed. The doctor started to say something rude in reply, but David cut him off smoothly.

"Yes," David said, "we are all very grateful to have Christy with us. She is an invaluable part of the mission. I don't know what we'd do without her."

"Probably wallow in ignorance while we drink corn liquor and shoot at each other."

Dr. MacNeill's quick, dry humor was lost on their hostess. "Exactly," Mrs. Barclay said.

Christy, David, and Neil exchanged amused glances.

"Now if you three will excuse me, I simply must borrow Christy. There are so many of her friends waiting to see her!" Before Christy could object, Mrs. Barclay had whisked her away.

Suddenly a group of familiar faces surrounded her— Jeanette Grady, a childhood friend; Mabel and Melissa Bentley, sisters who were old school friends; and Elizabeth Deerfield, who had been in the church choir with Christy. They crowded around Christy, chattering away at the same time.

"Christy, you have no idea what Terence Jones has been up to!"

"Christy, wait till I tell you what Martha Bates told me. You'll just die!"

"Christy, you simply have to come with me to this wonderful new dress shop in the square. They have all the latest fashions from Paris and New York!"

"Christy, it's so good to see you! Things just haven't been the same around here without you. And it's no secret that Lance Barclay has been missing you."

"Christy, have you heard the newest music? They call it ragtime. My father simply cannot stand it!"

It was like being caught up in a whirlwind. Christy was surrounded by silk and crystal, taffeta and silver, lace and polished mahogany. Everyone's hair was perfectly done up. Every face was clean and powdered. The air was filled with the scent of expensive perfume.

And then Christy happened to look down. She saw something that struck her as more noticeable than all the rest.

Everyone was wearing shoes.

In the Cove, even many of the adults went around barefoot, whatever the weather.

Christy felt a pang of guilt. Suddenly it seemed strange and wrong to be in a room filled with people wearing shoes.

She turned and looked for her friends. Her parents were nowhere in sight, but she soon located Neil and David and Ruby Mae. They stood bunched together in a corner. The three of them looked simple and rugged and weather beaten.

Christy felt as if she were being pulled in two directions. Part of her wanted to rush back to her friends from Cutter Gap. But these other people were her friends too. It would be ridiculous to ignore them simply because they came from the city rather than the mountains.

"Christy," a new voice said.

She turned to see Lance Barclay, handsome as ever. "It really is you! And even more beautiful than I remembered."

"Lance," Christy said. She put out her hand to shake his. He took her fingers, bowed, and gently kissed them.

"May I have the first dance?" he asked. "Unless, of course, you've already promised it to some other man."

Christy was caught off guard. She hadn't promised the first dance to anyone. "Um, no," she said. "I mean yes." She took a breath. "No, I haven't promised the first dance, and yes, I would be honored to save it for you."

As if on cue, the music brightened suddenly into a waltz. The shifting groups of people moved toward the edges of the room, opening a large dance area in the middle of the room.

"Shall we?" Lance asked, still holding Christy's hand.

Christy gave a little bow, then followed Lance toward the middle of the floor. He truly was quite a handsome young man. His blond hair was perfectly combed. His smile was bright. His tuxedo was immaculately tailored.

As they walked, Christy caught sight of David. He stood to one side, looking severe and awkward in his dark suit. It was the same one he wore on Sunday mornings when he preached. It was new, however. It had been a gift from his mother on her visit to Cutter Gap in May.

David was watching Christy with an expression of shock. Beside him, Neil seemed a trifle less awkward, but he looked even more out of place in his favorite tweed jacket. He held a glass and stared fixedly at the floor.

Christy felt a pang of regret. David had asked her to

marry him. And even Neil had made his feelings for Christy known. It must look to the two men as if she had dumped them in a corner.

But following on the heels of her regret and guilt came a second feeling: resentment. Why should she have to worry about what David and Neil thought? Sometimes she felt as if she spent every minute of every day worrying about what people might think or say. Every day in the Cove was a struggle to hold the respect of the suspicious mountain folk. Every day she had to worry about the feelings of dozens of difficult students in her class. Every day there were worries over money for school supplies, and worries about the diseases that stalked the mountains, and worries over the ever-present threat of moonshine-fueled violence. Worry, worry, worry! It seemed like a thousand years since she'd spent a worry-free night.

She was sick of worry. Tired of it. Wasn't she entitled to some ease and comfort? Wasn't she entitled to put on her best dress and dance?

Lance put his left arm around her waist and began to move them with the music. Round and round they swirled. And when the first dance was done, Christy accepted another with Lance. Between dances, they chatted with their Asheville friends about art and poetry and the traveling theater troupe that would arrive soon to perform Shakespeare's *Macbeth*. Lance asked her to go riding the next day, and she agreed.

It was late when the party began to break up. Christy found Ruby Mae in a corner, talking to a boy her own age.

"This here's Thomas Wolfe," Ruby Mae said. "Tom, this here's my teacher, Miz Christy. I been a-tellin' Tom all about folks in Cutter Gap," she added.

"I'd love to hear more," the boy said eagerly.

"But not tonight," Christy said. "I think it's rather late and we'd best all be getting home. Where are Rev. Grantland and Dr. MacNeill? Have you seen them?"

"Yes'm. They left some time back. Hours ago. I 'spect they were tuckered out. They both looked a might down."

"They left?" Christy asked in alarm. "They both left?"

"Yes, Miz Christy. They said they was a-goin' back to the house. They said I should remind you about Bessie having her operation tomorrow. If you was still interested."

"They said that? The part about if I was 'still interested'?"

"Yes," Ruby Mae said. "Although, factually speaking, it was the doctor what said it, and the preacher, he just nodded his head."

"As if I wouldn't care about Bessie," Christy said angrily. "Of course I'll be there."

Just then, Lance appeared at Christy's side. "You won't forget our date to go riding tomorrow, will you?"

"Of course not, Lance. I'll be there. Bessie's operation is at eight in the morning. I'll meet you at your stables at nine-thirty, just as we planned. That will leave plenty of time."

Eight

"I'm scared, Miz Christy," Bessie said. "If it didn't hurt so bad I wouldn't let no one cut into me. No how, no way."

Bessie was in her hospital bed, propped on starched white pillows. Her face looked pale and drawn. Her eyes were wide with fear. Ruby Mae and David stood nearby. David seemed unusually withdrawn to Christy—almost as if he were pouting.

"Do you reckon it hurts much when the doctor cuts into you?" Ruby Mae asked.

"Bessie won't feel a thing, I'm sure," Christy said. "The doctor will give you ether, Bessie, and you'll simply fall asleep. When you wake up, you'll start mending, and soon you'll be your old self again."

"Let's hope we'll all be our old selves again soon," David muttered darkly.

"What did you say, Preacher?" Bessie asked.

David sent Christy a sidelong look. "I was just making a comment about people being their old selves, Bessie. As opposed to turning into someone different just because they happen to find themselves in a different circumstance."

"I'm sure that would never happen to any of us," Christy said to David.

"Happens all the time," David said. "People change. Sometimes they change in the twinkling of an eye."

"No one has changed, David," Christy said with feeling. "Just because a person enjoys an evening relaxing and talking to old friends does not mean that person has changed."

"Ruby Mae?" Bessie whispered. "What are they goin' on about?"

"Miz Christy has herself a new beau," Ruby Mae said. "His name is Lance, and he's about the handsomest—"

"Aha! See?" David said. "Do you hear what Ruby Mae is saying?"

Just then Dr. MacNeill came in. He was wearing a white cotton coat over his regular clothing. "So how's the patient?" he asked Bessie.

"Hush, Doctor," Bessie said, "we're listenin' to Miz Christy and the preacher fussin' with each other."

"We are not fussing with each other, Bessie," Christy said. "Where did you ever get such an idea? We're here to see you and to keep you company."

"And you should be glad of it, Bessie." The doctor grinned. "Miss Huddleston has many demands on her time. It's generous of her to be here at all."

Christy was stung by the accusations of David and Neil. True, she had spent most of the previous evening with Lance and her old friends. But that was only normal, wasn't it? She hadn't seen any of them in a long time.

"Are you ready to start your operation, Doctor?" she asked. "Or are you too busy making unfair remarks about me?"

"No, I'm not ready," the doctor said. "Dr. Mecklen, who'll be assisting me, isn't here yet. He had an emergency across town and will be delayed."

"Delayed? For how long?" Christy asked.

"We should be able to start the operation by eight-thirty." Dr. MacNeill narrowed his eyes suspiciously. "Why? Do you have a pressing engagement?"

Christy tried to look nonchalant. "I was supposed to go riding with . . . with a friend . . . at nine-thirty."

"A friend," David repeated. "A friend, indeed. I'll wager you mean that Lance fellow."

"The young man with the greasy, perfumed hair?" Dr. MacNeill grinned again.

"That Miz Christy, she sure is somethin'!" Ruby Mae said to Bessie. "Now she's done got herself three fellers."

"I have done no such thing!" Christy protested.

"It's all right, Miz Christy," Bessie said helpfully. "I'll be fine if you have to go meet your new sweetheart."

"I do not have a new sweetheart," Christy said as forcefully as she could. "Lance Barclay is just an old friend."

"Is he kin to Granny Barclay?" Bessie asked.

"That hardly seems likely, Bessie," Christy said.

"On account of, see, Granny Barclay had a brother once what left Cutter Gap for the lowlands," Bessie explained.

"The Barclays are a very successful, very well-respected family in Asheville," Christy said. "I truly doubt they're related to—" She stopped suddenly. But it was too late. The snobbish, thoughtless words were out of her mouth.

"You were about to say, Christy?" David asked.

Dr. MacNeill's eyes had lost their twinkling amusement as he stared at Christy. "She was about to say that this powdered, pomaded, perfumed fellow Lance could hardly be related to a toothless old mountain woman who lives in a shack so tumbledown that Mr. Lance Barclay wouldn't stable a horse in it."

"That is not what I said, and it is certainly not what I meant," Christy said. "You're being unfair."

"Oh, are we?" the doctor muttered.

"You're embarrassed by us," David said. "Embarrassed by all of us."

"That is untrue!"

"Is it, Christy?" David asked. "Then answer this question: back in the Cove, Fairlight Spencer is your closest friend. She's a fine-looking woman, but she owns no more than two dresses, and both of them are faded and frayed. She owns only one old pair of shoes, and when she speaks, it's the twang of the mountains you hear. And I very much doubt if she has an opinion on the Paris fashions. So the question is, Christy, wouldn't you have been embarrassed to have Fairlight at that party last night?"

The question cut like a knife. How would Jeanette Grady and Elizabeth Deerfield and the Bentley sisters have treated Fairlight? Politely to her face, yes. But behind her back wouldn't they have tittered and smirked at her clothes and her hair and the way she spoke?

"Fairlight Spencer is my friend," Christy said, "wherever I am and whomever I'm with. And so are all of you. I'm sorry you think so little of me."

"You'll have to choose, you know," the doctor said darkly. "Sooner or later, you'll come to it. Are you a part of Cutter Gap and the mountains? Do you belong there? Truly belong?

Or are you just a decent young woman trying to do good among people you'll always keep at arm's length?"

For a while, no one spoke. The silence was finally broken by Dr. Mecklen's arrival. Bessie had to be prepared for surgery, and the two doctors had to go to the operating theater.

Christy waited in a small room with David and Ruby Mae. They prayed silently for Bessie's well-being. When they were done, Ruby Mae occupied herself looking through copies of *Harper's Bazaar*. Occasionally she would mutter "Well, I never!" or "Landsakes!" at something she saw in the magazine.

After a while, David joined Christy on the wooden bench where she sat. "You know, Christy, the doctor and I rarely agree on anything. But I have to admit, he has wisdom. I wonder if perhaps he is right. And . . ." He hesitated, as if uncertain of how to say what was in his heart. "I wonder if this isn't why you said no to my proposal of marriage?"

"What do you mean?" Christy asked.

"Was it just me you were refusing? Or were you saying no to the whole idea of a life in Cutter Gap? I wonder." He smiled wistfully. "I suppose I can't help but wonder if your reply might have been different if I were the pastor of a church here in Asheville rather than the minister for a tiny, struggling mission deep in the mountains."

"Of course that wasn't why I said no," Christy said. She looked into David's sad eyes. "David, I said no because I wasn't ready to make so large a decision. I have to be sure about marriage. Absolutely sure."

Dr. MacNeill appeared in the doorway. His white gown had smears of blood on it, but he was smiling. "Everything went perfectly. No problems at all. Bessie is fine. She'll be a bit sore for a few days, but she'll be good as new before you know it."

"Thank the Lord," David said.

"Yes, well, if I may say so, my technique had a little something to do with it," Dr. MacNeill said with a grin. "And Dr. Mecklen's as well."

"Can we go in and see her?" Christy asked.

"No, not yet. She won't wake up for another hour or so. Then I'm sure she'll want to see you."

Christy glanced at the clock. Nine-fifteen. *I should have left fifteen minutes ago*, she thought. *I gave my word to Lance, and he'll be waiting for me at the stables.* "I'm supposed to . . . I still have that appointment."

"Ah. The appointment," the doctor said meaningfully.

"I gave my word that I would meet him at nine-thirty. It would be terribly rude of me to stand him up. You said Bessie wouldn't be awake for an hour or so. I'll be back by then."

It made sense, Christy told herself. Despite the looks that David, Neil, and Ruby Mae were giving her, it did make sense. And yet, as she turned and walked from the room, a feeling of guilt pursued her.

Neil's words echoed in her mind. *"You'll have to choose, you know. Sooner or later, you'll come to it. Are you a part of Cutter Gap and the mountains? Do you belong there? Truly belong?"*

Nine

CHRISTY RUSHED BACK TO HER HOUSE TO CHANGE INTO her riding clothes. By the time she got to the Barclays' stables, she was fifteen minutes late for her meeting with Lance, but he didn't seem to mind.

"I'd happily wait for you all day," he said. "How is the young lady doing?"

"Bessie? Oh, she came through the operation just fine," Christy assured him. "But I'm afraid I can't spend much time with you, Lance. I want to be there when she wakes up."

"I understand perfectly," he said. "I just wanted to ride a ways and show you something I think will be of special interest to you."

The horse stable was behind the Barclay home. It housed four horses. Once, back when Christy was still a child, it had held twice that number. But that was before so many people began to own automobiles.

"I don't suppose you do much riding up in the hills," Lance said as they saddled their horses.

"Actually, the mission owns a beautiful black stallion we

call Prince. I ride him from time to time. Though many of the trails are so steep and narrow that they can only be traveled on foot."

"There are no roads, then?"

"Nothing that would be called a road here in Asheville," Christy admitted. "The cabins are spread so far and wide that connecting them all by roads would be hopelessly expensive. I'm afraid there are many more pressing concerns for the mountain people. Shoes, coats, medicine, school books."

She cinched the saddle tight. Lance came around to help her climb up. "I can manage, thank you," she said.

Lance smiled. "You've become very independent since moving away."

Christy swung easily up into the saddle. "I haven't had much choice about that, I'm afraid. I have a classroom of six-ty-seven children, ranging from the smallest to some so large they almost frighten me. I have to manage them every day. David . . . Mr. Grantland . . . helps out, as does Miss Alice Henderson from time to time. But generally I'm on my own."

Lance led the way out of the yard and down the road. "It worries me to think of you way back in those hills." He nodded in the direction of the Blue Ridge Mountains, a tall line that swept down and around Asheville. They were close enough to see, but with only their gentle foothills touching the city itself.

"Poverty. Violence. Sickness. Danger," Lance continued. "And no family and few friends for you to lean on in times of trouble."

Christy looked toward the skyline and frowned. Yes, she thought, there was violence and sickness and danger in those beautiful mountains. "I'm needed there," she said simply.

"I admire your feelings," Lance said. "But have you ever considered how your parents must feel? I know that they worry about you all the time."

Christy shifted uncomfortably. She had been expecting a simple, friendly ride. She'd imagined they would talk of old friends and good times. The conversation was taking a decidedly serious turn.

"I'm sorry if they worry," she said. "I try never to tell them anything in my letters that will upset them."

"Yes, but everyone knows what the mountain men are like," Lance said. "Just last week there was a trial for a moonshiner who had killed a revenue agent. It was in all the newspapers. The crime took place very near to Cutter Gap, I understand."

Christy nodded. "I know about it. It was actually ten miles from Cutter Gap."

"But there are blood feuds in the hills."

Christy could not deny the truth. Sometimes the mountain men settled their differences with guns. The fights were often over long-ago insults between clans. Even in Cutter Gap, some families—families who had drawn blood in the past—barely tolerated each other.

"The people are very poor," she said. "They've been forgotten by time and civilization, Lance. Faith and morality often weaken in the face of despair." She smiled wryly. "And evil is not entirely unknown here in Asheville."

"No, it isn't." Lance laughed. Then, more seriously, he said, "But still, here you would have your family, Christy."

"But there I have my mission."

"There are poor children here too," Lance said. "Look around you."

Without noticing, Christy had followed Lance into one of the poorer sections of town. It was a neighborhood of tar-paper shacks and rickety lean-tos in the shadow of one of the huge textile mills along the riverfront.

Ever since the railroad had come to Asheville in 1880, Asheville had grown rapidly. Mills and factories had been built. They had provided jobs to mountain people who came down from the hills. But often the jobs paid too little to allow a man to feed or house his family adequately.

"You see, there's poverty here too," Lance said.

"Yes," Christy admitted. "And so near to our own homes." Here, too, she saw children without shoes playing in the dirt. And here, too, defeated-looking men lounged in dark door-ways drinking from bottles of illegal whiskey.

"My father and I, and some of the other businessmen in town, are concerned for these folk," Lance said. "We pay our own workers a fair living wage. But I'm sorry to say that many businesses do not. A lot of these folks are in terrible shape."

He reined in his horse and looked Christy in the eye. "Christy, these people need help just as much as the people in the mountains. You can see that."

"Of course I can," she said softly.

"There's a group of us," Lance said. "My father and the others. We've begun meeting at the church on Wednesday nights. As you know, Rev. Grantland will be speaking to us tomorrow night. Originally, we'd planned to help with your mission."

"We would gladly accept any help offered," Christy said.

Lance looked uncomfortable. "Well, the fact is we've decided on something different." He pointed to a brand-new building. It was bare wood, not yet painted. "When that is done, it will be the start of our own mission. A mission to our own poor, right here in Asheville. That will be our school."

Christy was stunned—stunned and disappointed. If her church didn't help the Cutter Gap mission, there would be no new schoolbooks, no chalk, no pencils. Perhaps no more mission at all. But she knew she shouldn't be upset. If the church used its money to build this new mission, it would be wonderful for the needy people here.

Still, it was hard not to be heartsick at the possibility that her own mission might soon fail.

"Christy, we would like you to come with Rev. Grantland. We'd like you to tell us a little about your school."

"Me, give a speech?" Christy asked. The very thought made her throat clutch up. "What would I say?"

"Just tell us what you've done in Cutter Gap. Tell us what you've learned."

"I don't know what I've learned," Christy said helplessly. "Most days I don't think I've learned anything. Except to watch out when frightened hogs are running loose," she added with a laugh.

"Then tell us about the pigs," Lance said. He leaned over and put his hand on Christy's arm. "Christy, there are important missions to be done everywhere. Sometimes far away. Sometimes very close to home. Close to those who . . . who care for you."

Christy met his gaze and felt a familiar blush rising up her neck.

Then her eyes went wide. "Oh, no! Bessie! What time is it?"

They rode swiftly back to the stable, and Christy went straight to the hospital without taking time to change out of her riding clothes. But when she arrived she saw Neil leaving the hospital alone.

"Too late," the doctor said flatly. "She woke up and asked for you. But now she's asleep again, and I won't have her disturbed. She needs her rest."

"I hurried back . . ." Christy began lamely.

"Yes, I can see that."

His sarcasm hurt. It hurt all the more because he was right. She had let Bessie down. The very reason she had come to Asheville was to take care of Bessie. Now she had failed.

"I'll apologize to her," Christy said. "I . . . I had other things on my mind. I became distracted."

"Yes, I know it can be very distracting riding around town, nodding to all the fine gentle-men and ladies. Parading around in your fancy riding habit with that young squirt."

"Neil, I am desperately sorry that I wasn't there for Bessie when she opened her eyes. I feel terrible about it. But I wasn't parading anywhere. And I really think you would do us both a favor to keep your feelings of jealousy separate from your concern for Bessie."

"Jealousy?" the doctor said a little too loudly. "Me, jealous of that . . . that . . . fop? Hah!"

"If it isn't jealousy, Doctor, then how else do you explain your contempt for a man you know nothing about? You're not usually so closeminded." She gave him a cold smile. "On the contrary, you're usually the very soul of tolerance."

The doctor sputtered as though he might have something to say in reply, but in the end he merely grumbled, "Don't go disturbing my patient."

"Of course I won't disturb your patient. But I will go inside and wait quietly by her bed, so that when she does awaken again, I'll be there."

The doctor had no reply. He slammed his hat on his head and stormed off, muttering, "Jealous! Of that over-moneyed puppy?"

Christy headed into the hospital. She found Bessie still asleep, with Ruby Mae at her side.

Ruby Mae popped up out of her chair as soon as Christy appeared. "Miz Christy! How did your ride go with Mr. Lance?"

"It went fine, Ruby Mae," Christy said. "How is Bessie?"

"Oh, she's doin' good. What happened with you and Mr. Lance? Did he up and propose to you?"

"Ruby Mae, where on earth did you ever get such an idea?" Christy demanded.

Ruby Mae nodded wisely. "Oh, I seen the way he looked at you at the jollification last night."

"Did he try and kiss you?" a weak voice asked.

Both Christy and Ruby Mae spun around in surprise. It was Bessie, wide awake.

"Bessie! You're supposed to be asleep," Christy cried.

"I had to wake up to hear about you and this Lance feller, Miz Christy. Ruby Mae says he ain't quite as pretty as the preacher, and ain't quite as smart as the doctor, but he's more like a mixin' of both of them."

Christy had to laugh. She shook her finger at her two students. "You girls need to learn to stay out of other people's business. What a pair of old gossips you are! You could give Granny O'Teale lessons."

"Are you going to marry Mr. Lance if'n you stay here in Asheville?" Bessie asked.

Christy frowned. "What do you mean, 'if I stay here in Asheville'? Where did you get that notion?"

Bessie and Ruby Mae exchanged a long glance. "I kinda happened to overhear the preacher and Dr. MacNeill talkin'," Ruby Mae said. "They was sayin' as how you'd probably never go back to Cutter Gap, on account of how much easier life is here in Asheville."

"They said that?" Christy demanded. "They have no right to say those kinds of things!"

The two girls were staring at her solemnly. "Is it true, though, Miz Christy?" Ruby Mae asked softly.

No, Christy wanted to say. *No, it's a ridiculous idea. Of course I'm going back to the Cove.* But something held her back. She hesitated. And she was shocked by her own hesitation.

Was she really considering not going back to Cutter Gap? She hadn't even formed the idea in her head, at least not consciously. But now that Ruby Mae had posed the question, the answer was not so easy.

"I have every intention of returning to Cutter Gap," Christy said evasively.

From their worried expressions, it was easy to see that neither Ruby Mae nor Bessie was convinced.

Ten

THE NEXT DAY, RUBY MAE WOKE EARLY. SHE USUALLY GOT up with the sun. Back home at the mission, she had morning chores to do. But here in Miz Christy's house, there were no chores. Leastways, no one had asked her to do anything.

Miz Christy had promised to take her shopping after they went to visit Bessie. And of course they would get something for Bessie as well. But when Ruby Mae climbed out of bed and went out into the hallway, she found her teacher's door still shut. The doctor and the preacher were both still asleep too.

She headed downstairs. The feel of the carpeted stairs on her bare feet was amazing. It must be a mighty fine thing to wake up on a cold morning and be able to walk on rugs. She'd never even heard of the like before.

She followed a delicious smell toward the kitchen. There she found Miz Christy's mama pulling a pan of fresh biscuits from the oven.

"Ah, Ruby Mae, good morning," Mrs. Huddleston said cheerfully. "I see you're an early riser like me."

"Yes, ma'am," Ruby Mae said. "Mostly, that is. Sometimes I lay abed till the sun is almost up over the ridge."

"Would you care for a biscuit? And perhaps some tea or coffee?"

"I wouldn't want to impose on you, ma'am," Ruby Mae said. But the biscuits did look awfully good. And she had a powerful hunger.

"Nonsense. I was just making coffee. And I baked these biscuits to be eaten. Come, have a seat. I've been meaning to have a talk with you."

Ruby Mae took a chair and watched with wide eyes as Mrs. Huddleston piled the biscuits high on a plate. Then she brought out sweet cream and fresh butter and two kinds of fruit preserves, orange and boysenberry.

It was a regular feast, and Ruby Mae dug right in. "This biscuit is a pure taste of heaven, Mrs. Huddleston, it truly is."

"That's very kind of you." Mrs. Huddleston grinned. "Ever since we lost Mathilda, I've been doing all the cooking. I'm afraid biscuits are the only thing I cook really well."

"Was Mathilda kin of yours?"

"Oh, no, she was our servant. She did a lot of the house-work and some of the cooking as well. She finally got married and now takes care of her own family."

"A servant?"

"Yes. You know, she helped out and lived with us. She was almost a part of the family. I wish I could find someone to replace her."

Mrs. Huddleston was looking straight at Ruby Mae, like maybe she was thinking on something. Nervous, Ruby Mae checked the front of her dress to see if she'd spilled some jam or crumbs.

"So, tell me about your life in Cutter Gap," Mrs. Huddleston said. "I know that you live at the mission house with Christy. Do you enjoy living there?"

"Oh, yes, ma'am. We get plenty to eat, and on cold nights there's a small fire and all. Of course, it's nothing near so fine as this house."

Mrs. Huddleston nodded. "And how do you like having Christy as a teacher?"

"Miz Christy is purely the best teacher in the whole world. Most everyone loves her. Except for some folks that don't like outsiders. And the moonshiners, they don't like her much, since she and the preacher spoke against them. There's some folks say she and the preacher and even Miz Alice should go back to where they come from and leave well enough alone."

"And how does Dr. MacNeill feel about the mission? And Christy?"

Ruby Mae hid a smile. Now they were getting around to what Mrs. Huddleston really wanted to talk about. "The doctor? He says he doesn't really approve of the mission, but that's just what he says. If you know what I mean, ma'am. It ain't the mission he doesn't want around, it's mostly the preacher."

"I see. So Rev. Grantland and Dr. MacNeill don't get along?"

Ruby Mae wondered if she should say anything more. But like Miss Ida was always saying, Ruby Mae did like to talk. "I reckon you already heard me say that the preacher and the doctor is both sweet on Miz Christy," she said.

"Yes, and I'd already guessed as much," Mrs. Huddleston said with a smile. "I wonder, though . . . Surely Dr. MacNeill could establish a practice somewhere else. Say, in a city. Right here in Asheville, even. And Rev. Grantland could no doubt find a church in need of an eager young preacher."

Ruby Mae swallowed the last crumbs of biscuit. Then she looked up at Mrs. Huddleston. "I reckon they could. If 'n they wanted to."

Mrs. Huddleston sighed. "To be honest with you, Ruby Mae, I miss my daughter. I wish I could find a way to convince her to come home. But I fear that Rev. Grantland and Dr. MacNeill are giving her powerful reasons to stay in the mountains."

"I don't think the doctor would ever leave the mountains," Ruby Mae said. "He's born and raised in those mountains, even though he did go away to learn his medicine in some faraway place. He come back to the mountains, and I 'spect he'll stay."

"I see."

"But I calculate as how the preacher will leave someday. He's not from the mountains at all. I figure there will come a day when he says, 'I done my work here. It's time to move on.'"

"So if my daughter chooses Rev. Grantland, I may be able to see her move back to Asheville and raise her family here where I can see them grow up. But if she chooses Dr. Mac-Neill, I'll see her only rarely." Mrs. Huddleston leaned across the table and said in a low voice, "You're a bright girl, Ruby Mae. Whom do you think she will choose?"

Ruby Mae smiled. She had a pretty good idea which man Miz Christy liked better—even if Miz Christy wasn't sure herself. At least Ruby Mae had been sure before she came with Miz Christy to Asheville. Now she wasn't sure of anything.

"If it was a straight-up choice betwixt the preacher and

the doctor," Ruby Mae began, "I'd have to say Miz Christy would —"

"Good morning," Christy said loudly as she entered the room.

Ruby Mae and Mrs. Huddleston both jumped at the sound of her voice.

Christy looked from one to the other. "I believe my ears are burning. If I didn't know better, I'd swear there'd been some gossiping going on here."

"Gossiping?" Mrs. Huddleston said. "What a thought! No, I was just talking to Ruby Mae. You see, I was just about to make her an offer."

"An offer?" Christy repeated.

"Yes. I was about to ask Ruby Mae whether she would like to come and live here permanently. She could take over some of Mathilda's work. I could really use the help."

Ruby Mae's mouth dropped open. And so did Christy's.

⁓

June 11, 1912

I have just come from the hospital. Bessie is fine and in good spirits.

I wish I could say the same for David and Neil. Especially David. I told him about our church's plans to start their own mission. He knows now that they will not be able to help him with the mission at Cutter Gap. Naturally, he said he wished them all the best. But I know he is disappointed. It was not what he had hoped for. But nothing is turning out quite the way we all had hoped.

Here I am, home again in Asheville. Among people I've known for many years. It's good to be with my family and to sleep in my old bed. But somehow I don't feel the way I thought I would.

Nothing seems quite right. I feel as if all that should be most familiar has become strange. Neil and David both seem to be angry at me. Perhaps they are jealous that I have spent some time with Lance. But Lance is just an old, dear friend. There is no reason for David or Neil to be jealous.

Or is there? There was a time, back when Lance and I were little children playing together, that we said we would be married when we grew up. That's just the prattle of little children, and doesn't mean anything. But still, I believe Lance does have some feeling for me.

Ruby Mae, too, is acting differently toward me. Or is it that I am behaving differently toward her?

And even though everything here in Asheville should seem familiar and welcoming to me, it seems changed somehow. Perhaps it is I who have changed. Perhaps once you've left, you can never really go home again.

I only know that I am confused. I no longer feel certain of where I belong. I care deeply for my students and Fairlight Spencer and Miss Alice back at Cutter Gap. But my family is here in Asheville.

Too many questions are swimming around in my head. What are my true feelings for Neil and David and Lance? What are my true feelings about Cutter Gap and Asheville?

I suppose it all comes down to one question: where do I belong? I was certain that God had led me to the mission in Cutter Gap. But now that I am back here, I wonder if He has not shown me a new way—a way that brings me back to my family.

Tonight I am to speak to the meeting of businessmen organized by Lance and his father at our church. I think I know what they are going to ask of me. And I don't know what answer to give.

All I ever wanted was to help people, to make a difference in people's lives. How am I to do that? Where am I to do that?

My church here will give no help to the Cutter Gap mission because they are building their own mission. Without that help, the mission that Miss Alice founded may fail.

Against that, there may be the chance to do wonderful work right here in Asheville. Thanks to mother's offer, I could even keep Ruby Mae with me. But what about David? And Neil?

David and Neil think I will be influenced by the comforts of home. And I must admit, if I am honest, that I do enjoy those comforts. But I hope I can set aside such unworthy considerations and find the way to do God's will.

I feel as if I am caught up in a tornado, being spun wildly around with David and Neil and Lance, with the poor children of Cutter Gap, and the poor children of Asheville; with my parents and Miss Alice and Fairlight; and, yes, with my warm, comfortable room.

It's all too much. I pray that God will show me the way, because I am unable to find it alone.

Eleven

IT MAY INTEREST YOU TO KNOW, REVEREND, THAT THE bells in our steeple were cast by the same foundry that fashioned the Liberty Bell." Mr. Barclay, Lance's father, had David by the arm and was showing him around the church. They were waiting for all the members of the businessmen's association to assemble in a meeting room off the church.

Lance was with them too. Christy was careful to avoid seeming overly friendly to either David or Lance. The last thing she needed was to have either man feeling jealous.

"We have almost fifteen hundred in our congregation now," Mr. Barclay said. "Many of the most prominent citizens of Asheville. You'll meet some wealthy and influential men here tonight."

Christy felt a little sorry for David. Mr. Barclay was justly proud of the church, but she worried that David might be feeling a little overwhelmed.

"That must be an awesome burden for your pastor," David said. "Our congregation is quite a bit smaller. In fact, I believe we could fit most of them in the first two pews of this church and have room left over."

"Don't you find it frustrating sometimes, having so small a flock when you are obviously such a bright and energetic young man?" Mr. Barclay asked. "There's always a place for a smart fellow like yourself here."

"I feel that God led me to do His work at the Cutter Gap mission, Mr. Barclay." David laughed easily. "Perhaps the Lord has a less complimentary opinion of my abilities than you have."

"In any event," Lance said smoothly, "no congregation could ever seem poor that had Miss Huddleston as a member." He gave a little bow in Christy's direction.

"Indeed," David agreed a little frostily.

Christy pretended not to have heard either man.

Besides, her thoughts were on more serious matters. She was troubled by David's easy confidence that he was doing the right thing by staying at the mission. How could David be so sure of his calling? She wished she could be that confident.

Christy looked around at the church. She had been baptized in this building. She had first taken Holy Communion here.

She thought of the church in the mountains. It was easy to recall every detail, since it was also her schoolroom. The altar was her desk. The pews were supplemented with her student's desks. And the hogs snorted in the mud beneath the building on Sundays, the same as every other day.

"I believe we are about ready, Christy," Lance said, breaking into her thoughts.

"Oh. I'm sorry, I guess I was daydreaming."

"Now, don't be nervous," Mr. Barclay counseled. "These

men all want to hear what you and Rev. Grantland have to say. You know that we hope to reach out to our own poor, right here in Asheville. You two are the experts, so we'll listen very carefully."

The meeting consisted of almost a hundred men, all wearing conservative business suits and looking rather intimidating. After David spoke for a few minutes, explaining the purpose of the mission and its importance to the mountain folk, it was Christy's turn. She said a quick, silent prayer, then walked shakily to the podium.

She faced a sea of whiskers and waistcoats and skeptical looks. Then she saw Lance's face. He smiled encouragingly. And David gave her a little wink.

"Gentlemen, my name is Christy Huddleston. I suppose some of you know my family. We—"

"Speak up!" someone yelled out. "I can't hear her."

In a louder voice, Christy went on. "My name is Christy Huddleston. I am the teacher at the mission school of Cutter Gap. We have sixty-seven students, all in one classroom. I teach all the subjects except math and Bible studies, which Rev. Grantland takes care of. The students range across all ages. Some are almost as old as I am. A few had some schooling before the mission opened. Others had very little or none at all."

For ten minutes Christy told them all she could think of about the school and the students. But soon she began to wonder whether she was simply rambling on. She faltered.

"I . . . I don't know what else I can tell you," she said.

An old gentleman raised his voice. "Do you think that similar schools, combining all sorts of different students, could be made to work in other places?"

Christy shrugged. "I'm sure they could. I believe that most children want to learn, given the chance. It's not just a matter of having new books and desks and fine buildings—although we could certainly use those," she added with a self-conscious laugh. "But the truly important thing is simply to give the children the chance to learn. They will seldom disappoint you."

Mr. Barclay stood and joined her on the podium. "As you know, Miss Huddleston, we've been discussing the possibility of establishing a sort of mission to the many poor and uneducated families that have come to Asheville to work in the mills. Many have come down from the mountains in search of work. Others are from foreign countries and speak very little English. They need medical care and a school for their children."

"Yes, I think it sounds like a wonderful idea," Christy said enthusiastically.

"We have already put up a school building. But a school needs more than a building and desks. More, even, than students, be they ever so willing to learn. A school needs a teacher."

Christy tried to keep a smile plastered on her face. She knew what was coming next. She caught David's eye and could tell that he was filled with concern.

"A school needs a teacher," Mr. Barclay repeated. "One with experience in doing a great deal with very little. A teacher accustomed to working almost alone. A teacher with experience in large classrooms full of diverse children. In short, Miss Huddleston, what our school needs is you."

After the meeting was over, David and Christy walked back to her parents' home. For a while they were silent. Christy tried not to think, but simply enjoy the evening, as lights came on in the windows of the houses they passed and street lights glowed yellow. A mix of automobiles and horse-drawn wagons passed, dodging around the careening streetcars. Other couples were out walking as well. They smiled politely, the gentlemen tipping their hats. The moon was just appearing in a violet sky.

"I suppose I'll have to consider how the mission will replace you," David said at last. He sounded tense and clipped.

"What?" Christy said in surprise.

"I need to consider finding a teacher to replace you," David said. "I assume you will accept their offer."

"Well, I don't assume any such thing," Christy said.

"Nonsense," David said with surprising force. "The offer has everything in its favor. You would have a beautiful new classroom. Those gentlemen will see that you have all the school books and supplies you could ever want. No more sharing battered books with half the pages gone. No more worrying that you'll run out of everything. No more hostile, suspicious community. No more dealing with superstition and foolishness. No more hogs under the classroom."

"Do you honestly believe I would be swayed by new books?"

David smiled crookedly. "No," he admitted. "I don't think you could be swayed by a promise of new books. But I think you could be swayed by the chance to do important work while being close to your family and friends."

"David, I don't know what to do," Christy admitted.

"You would be rid of me if you stayed here."

Christy stopped walking. She put her hand on David's arm. "David, whatever I do, you have to know one thing: I have no desire to be rid of you."

"Really?" he asked. "You turned down my offer of marriage, after all."

"That was for other reasons," Christy said. "And I never said no. I just said I wasn't ready."

"And now you are ready to return to Asheville," he said bitterly.

"David, I just don't know. I . . . I felt that God led me to Cutter Gap. Might He not be leading me back here now?"

David hung his head. "I've wondered that same thing," he admitted. "Is this your true mission? To be here and help the community where you grew up? To do God's work and still have your family around you?" He shook his head. "There's no doubt that this school for the mill workers is a wonderful idea. And there's no doubt that you would be the best possible teacher they could ever hope to have. Am I just putting my own selfish interests ahead of God's will?"

"How can I know what is right?" Christy pleaded with him. "Tell me, David, and I will do whatever you decide."

David laughed gently. "No, Christy. It's not my decision to make, much as I would like to have you return with me to Cutter Gap. It is your decision. God will guide you."

Christy looked off toward the west. The sun had set behind the Blue Ridge Mountains, turning them into a dark silhouette. They seemed so far away, so alien.

It would be cold at the mission right now. If she were there, she would be grading papers, squinting in the dim light of the tiny lamp she allowed herself. There would be no big roaring fire, just a small one on the coldest nights. The shadows in the trees would be close about, isolating the mission. She would go to her lumpy, cold bed and listen to the wind and the howls of distant wolves. And she would never be sure that she was safe from the dangerous moonshiners who plied their trade in the night.

Here there was light. Light everywhere she looked. Her mother would have a late supper of roast beef and fresh-baked bread and sharp cheese waiting for her when she got home. Afterward, they would sit by a cheery fire and read or talk. And then she would go up to a feather bed, secure and peaceful.

Was it necessary to suffer in order to do good? No, that was vanity. The children of the mill workers needed a teacher just as much as the children of the mountains.

David had said that God would give her guidance. She hoped he was right. Tomorrow morning they were all to take the train back to El Pano, and then it would be on to Cutter Gap.

Whatever she decided to do, she would be on that train. The school year was not over yet. And she would at least have to say goodbye.

Twelve

CHRISTY WAS AWAKE LONG BEFORE DAWN. IN FACT, SHE HAD been lying awake in bed for hours by the time she heard a distant rooster crow, signaling the rise of the sun.

She had prayed many times for an answer to her dilemma. But she still felt uncertain and unsettled. One way or the other, she knew she would be getting on the train to El Pano with the others. Whatever her decision was, she had to return to Cutter Gap, even if it was only to get her things and say goodbye.

While she waited for the rest of the household to awaken, she packed her bags. When she smelled the familiar aromas of coffee and biscuits coming up the stairs, she went down. She found her mother and Ruby Mae in the kitchen. Ruby Mae was assisting in the preparation of a new batch of biscuits.

"Good morning, sweetheart," Christy's mother said.

"Ruby Mae, are you learning your new duties? Does this mean you've decided to stay here?" Christy wondered aloud. Maybe Ruby Mae's decision would help with her own.

"Oh, no, Miz Christy," Ruby Mae said. "I was just a-learnin' your mama's recipe so I can fetch up a batch of these biscuits when I get back home. Won't Miss Ida be surprised?"

"Yes, I suppose she will," Christy said.

"I am very disappointed that Ruby Mae won't be staying here," Mrs. Huddleston said. "The house will seem so empty with both of you gone again."

"Miz Christy will be back soon, though," Ruby Mae said.

"Is that true, dear?" Mrs. Huddleston asked eagerly.

Christy was flustered. "Ruby Mae, I haven't decided whether that's true or not." She looked helplessly at her mother. "I'm sorry, Mother. But I'm still not sure. I just don't know."

"Whatever you decide, your father and I will support you," she said. "But of course you know how we feel. It would mean everything to us to have you back home."

"Yes, Mother, I know."

Just then Christy's father entered, followed by David and Neil. The three of them stood stock still and stared expectantly at Christy.

"I don't know!" she said, exploding in frustration.

"Now, everyone leave Christy alone," Mrs. Huddleston said. "There are hot biscuits and coffee. Eggs and ham will be along in a moment or two."

"I'll have to make do with just a biscuit, I'm afraid," Dr. MacNeill said. "I've got to get over to the hospital to make sure Bessie's ready."

"I'll come with you," Christy said quickly.

"No need," the doctor said. "She's no longer to be your concern, is she?"

Christy felt anger rising in her. Everyone seemed so sure that she'd already made her decision. She followed the doctor out into the parlor, out of hearing of the others. "I have not decided yet, Neil. And as of this moment, Bessie Coburn is still my responsibility as much as yours."

"Responsibility? That's rich, coming from you. A responsibility is something you can't just walk away from."

Christy tried to rein in her frustration. The doctor always seemed to bring out the worst in her. "Neil, you're a doctor, and so you have certain responsibilities. If you were faced with a choice between helping a patient you knew for certain could be saved or helping a patient who might be beyond help, what would you do?"

The doctor fidgeted and looked away. "Are you telling me you think the Cutter Gap mission may really have to shut down?"

"I don't know," Christy said. "Miss Alice never seems to worry. David is concerned, I think. I had hoped to get some contributions from my church here in Asheville. But now it seems they have their own mission to support."

The doctor was silent for a moment. At last he said, "The answer to your question, Christy, is that if I had to choose between helping those who can be helped and those who can't, I'd have to help those who can be helped. But," he added, "I'd first make very certain that someone was beyond help before I walked away."

"Even if the Cutter Gap mission survives, why choose to do my work there rather than here? I am needed just as much here. What if it turned out, Doctor, that both your patients could be helped, but you only had the time and ability to help one?" Christy searched his face as if he might really have the answer.

The doctor smiled. "I guess sometimes you just do the best you can and pray."

He'd said it as a sort of joke. Christy knew that the doctor did not pray. Or at least, if he did, he denied doing so. And yet his answer was perfect.

"Do the best you can and pray," Christy repeated softly.

⸺

Christy wiped tears from her eyes as the train pulled away from the Asheville station. She waved through the window to her parents, who stood on the platform.

Bessie Coburn was sitting across the aisle with Ruby Mae. Ruby Mae was busily telling Bessie all about Asheville and automobiles and the Huddlestons' fine house.

"I missed out on everything," Bessie complained. "Although I reckon just being rid of that terrible pain is enough for me. I feel so good I could run all the way back to Cutter Gap!"

"No running, Bessie," Dr. MacNeill said sternly. "Not for at least a month. If I find out you've been doing any running, jumping, skipping, or heavy chores and you ruin my beautiful stitches, I warn you, I will not be happy."

Bessie grinned. "I would never do nothin' to ruin your stitchwork, Doctor. Why, it's almost as fine as my mama's quiltin'."

"What?" David said in mock horror. "Only 'almost'? Dr. MacNeill, running second place to Lety Coburn's quilting stitches?"

Christy smiled, despite herself. The train picked up speed, and soon she could feel the drag of gravity as they began to climb back up the mountains. Soon they were high on the mountain's side, crawling along the narrow ledge above a precipice.

"We'll be home soon," Ruby Mae said to Bessie.

"Home," Bessie agreed. "Traveling is good, but home is best. Isn't that right, Miz Christy?"

"Yes, it is," Christy said. She sent Bessie a smile. But then her mood darkened again. *Yes, home was best*, she thought. But she wasn't going home; she was leaving home. Again. Her home was behind her. Her friends, her family, all back in Asheville.

What was she to do?

"Do the best you can and pray." The doctor's words came back to her.

Christy closed her eyes. She tried to shut out the sounds of conversation all around her. She tried to quiet the voice of her own will, her own demands. *What am I to do? How am I to choose between home and Cutter Gap?*

She opened her eyes and looked across the aisle at Bessie and Ruby Mae gossiping. Ruby Mae was dressed once again in her own simple, homespun hand-me-downs.

Christy looked at David. He was deep in thought. His handsome face was clouded with concern, and she knew all the reasons for his worry. Would the mission survive? Would Christy stay or go?

Then she looked at the doctor. He was reading a medical journal and trying to look nonchalant. But his eyes weren't on the pages. He was staring blankly out at the sheer drop below.

I wish Miss Alice were here, Christy thought. *When I get home, I must ask her advice.*

When I get home?

Christy smiled.

Screeeeeech!

It was a sound like a saw going through metal. Christy could feel a shuddering vibration rattle the entire train.

Screeeeech!

Outside the window, Christy saw sparks being thrown up from the brakes. A man walking in the aisle was suddenly tossed forward, knocked to the floor at Christy's feet. Christy herself was thrown hard against the seat in front of her. Handbags and luggage flew over her head. The air was filled with a thousand grinding, ripping, tearing sounds, all at once.

Screams! People all around were screaming! The train car tilted far over to the left, then lurched heavily back to the right. Then . . . *Boom!* The car turned over. Up was down and down was up. Christy fell to the ceiling. Then the floor jumped back up and hit her. Bodies were being tossed everywhere, like straws in a tornado.

The car slammed against a tree. One entire side was peeled away, like the skin of a banana. Cold wind blasted in.

Christy felt herself flying through the air.

Thirteen

CHRISTY FLEW, WEIGHTLESS, THROUGH THE AIR. SHE FELL, down, down, down. But when she hit, her landing was soft. Thick bushes had cushioned her fall.

She took a deep breath—a gasp, really. She was still alive! Alive and surrounded by flowers. It seemed ridiculous somehow.

She struggled to her feet. All her limbs were still working, and she breathed a sigh of relief.

But as she looked around, her relief was short lived.

The entire train was off the tracks. Fortunately, none of the cars had gone over the edge of the cliff. But half the car she had been riding in dangled precariously over the side of the cliff. Most of one entire side had been peeled back to reveal the interior.

Christy gasped.

"Are you all right, Christy?" It was David. He came hobbling over to her. His ankle had been badly twisted. He took her in his arms and held her close.

"Yes, I'm fine," Christy said. She raised her voice to a shout. "Ruby Mae? Bessie? Neil?"

"Miz Christy? Help!"

"That's Ruby Mae's voice," Christy said.

David pointed. "It came from over there."

Christy rushed over, followed more slowly by David. They found Ruby Mae wedged between two big rocks. She was unhurt, but stuck.

"I cain't get loose, Miz Christy!" Ruby Mae wailed.

"Here, let me help you," Christy said. She tugged and pushed at the rocks. They were too big to move much, but it only took an inch to allow Ruby Mae to wiggle free.

"Christy!" Dr. MacNeill came rushing over. His left arm appeared to have been hurt. It dangled limply at his side.

"Neil!" Christy cried in relief.

"Doctor," David said. "Thank God you're alive. Is your arm hurt?"

"A simple fracture," the doctor said. "Painful, but not dangerous."

"Bessie," Christy said. "Where is Bessie?"

They scanned the faces of the others who had climbed or crawled from the train car. Up and down the tracks, people were walking around aimlessly, looking stunned. Some were bleeding. Some were crying out in pain and fear.

"We have to find Bessie," Christy said.

Just then they heard a pitiable cry. "Help me. Someone, please, help me!"

Christy froze. It was Bessie's voice. It had come from inside the train car—the train car that even now dangled over the precipice.

"Bessie! Hold on!" Ruby Mae cried.

"I'll go in and get her," David said.

"I doubt you can, not with that ankle," the doctor said.

"Better than you with that arm," David said. "Besides, Neil, you're probably the only doctor here, and there are people who need medical help. If something happens . . ." David managed a brave smile. "Better I go over the edge of that cliff than you, Doctor."

"Someone help me!" Bessie wailed again.

David turned away quickly and hobbled toward the car. A strong gust of wind blew up the valley. Christy saw the rail car tilt, as if it would plunge off the edge. She held her breath. The car came back to rest. But it was balanced as precariously as a teeter-totter.

David reached the car and rested against the jagged, torn opening. He started to hoist himself up, but then his grip failed and he fell back. He landed hard on his already strained foot.

"Ahhh," he moaned in pain.

Suddenly, without even thinking about it, Christy found herself running forward. She raced to David's side and helped him into a sitting position on a rock.

"You can't do this," she said. "Not with that leg. I'll go."

"Absolutely not!" David said.

"Christy! Get back here," the doctor yelled. "That car could slip over the side at any moment."

"Yes, I know. That's why we don't need any more weight in there than absolutely necessary. And I am smaller than either of you."

"I absolutely forbid it!" David said.

"So do I!" the doctor said.

"Wonders never cease!" Christy said. "That's the second

time this week the two of you have agreed on something." Then, ignoring them, she called out, "I'm coming, Bessie!"

She clambered up through the torn hole. The floor was tilted at a crazy angle. And as she stood up inside, she could feel the unsteadiness of the entire car.

When she looked around, her heart sank. Bessie lay at the far end of the car—the far end of a teeter-totter that might need only the weight of one young woman to send it crashing over to certain death.

"Bessie? I'm here," Christy said. "I'm right here."

"Miz Christy? Is that you?" Bessie moaned.

"Yes, Bessie. Can you move?"

"No, ma'am. The seat has got me pinned down. It's all twisted around so's I can't move an inch."

"Are you hurt?"

"No, I don't think so," Bessie said. "I just ain't got the strength to get free. Help me, Miz Christy."

Christy took two small steps forward. The floor tilted forward. Christy froze.

What should she do? Bessie was crying for help. But if she moved forward, she might be making a fatal mistake.

It might be that Bessie couldn't be helped.

Forward or backward? What was the right thing to do?

"Do the best you can and pray," Christy whispered.

"What did you say, Miz Christy?" Bessie asked.

"I said . . . I said I'm coming, Bessie. I'm coming."

Christy took a deep breath. *Please, God, let this be the right choice.* She walked forward, as slowly as she could. Halfway to Bessie, she felt the floor tilt further down. But Christy kept going. One step after another. Inch by careful inch. At last, after what seemed like hours, she reached Bessie's side.

"I'm here, Bessie," she said.

"I'm sorry to put you to the trouble, Miz Christy."

Christy almost laughed. Almost. She put her hands around the twisted metal bar that held Bessie down and pulled with all her might. Slowly, slowly, the bar moved. Then, suddenly, it pulled away.

Bessie was free!

"I reckon we best get out of here," Bessie said.

"I quite agree," Christy said.

She helped Bessie to her feet. Together they hobbled up the slanted aisle toward fresh air and safety. David and Neil and Ruby Mae were all anxiously waiting for them. They helped Bessie down to the firm ground. Christy climbed down, too, and breathed a huge sigh of relief.

The instant her feet touched the ground, she heard a scrunching, crushing sound. The near end of the rail car tilted wildly up in the air.

"There it goes!" David cried.

And with that the rail car went over the side of the cliff and disappeared. For a long moment, the world was still. Then there came a tremendous boom as the car hit bottom.

"You was almost kilt!" Ruby Mae cried.

The doctor was squinting skeptically. "That makes no sense at all. It should have fallen over when your combined weight was on the far end. When you went to get Bessie, it should have overbalanced."

Christy nodded. "Yes, that would make sense, Neil. And yet . . . that's not what happened. I wasn't sure if I should walk the length of that car to Bessie or not. I thought I might kill us both, and that would have made no sense at all. And yet my heart told me the right thing was to go to her. So I did."

"How on earth did you know it was the right thing?" the doctor demanded. "I'm telling you it makes no logical sense."

"Maybe sometimes right is just right, even if it doesn't make any logical sense," Christy said thoughtfully. She sent the doctor an impish grin. "Or maybe, Neil, we humble human beings don't always know what makes real sense. And then we can only listen for another voice. A voice that speaks to our hearts and guides us in the right direction. In other words, I did the best I could and prayed."

⌐#⌐

For the next few hours, Christy and David helped Dr. Mac-Neill see to the injured. Miraculously, no one had been seriously hurt. There were broken legs and bruises and strains, but nothing more serious. They'd found Dr. MacNeill's medical bag tossed from the train. That and makeshift bandages and splints were sufficient to the need.

It took two hours for help to reach them. When it finally arrived, it came from both directions. A small steam engine came uphill from Asheville. It carried volunteers sent to help. In addition, riders on horses came downhill from the direction of El Pano.

"Is that Miss Alice?" David wondered.

Christy squinted. "It is! Although I shouldn't be surprised. Wherever there's trouble and folks need help, that's where you'll find her."

"Not unlike another woman I know," David said, smiling at Christy.

"Good heavens," Dr. MacNeill said, looking in the other direction. "It's that young pup, Lance Barclay. And his father."

The two Barclay men were among the dozen volunteer

rescuers who had come up from Asheville on a spare loco-motive. They came rushing over as soon as their train had stopped.

Just moments later Miss Alice arrived and was glad to see her friends were all well. "I was in El Pano when we learned that the train was late and possibly wrecked. I came to help treat the injured. But I see the three of you have taken care of everything."

"Yes, a most amazing little field hospital," Mr. Barclay agreed. "We received a call from El Pano that something must have happened to the train."

"We were terribly worried about you, Christy," Lance said. "About all of you, I should say."

"Yes, I'm sure," David said dryly.

"Well, we didn't want to lose our new teacher," Lance said.

Miss Alice's eyebrows shot up. "New teacher?" She looked scarchingly at Christy.

"Yes, Christy is considering taking a position at the new mission school in Asheville," David explained.

"Indeed?" Miss Alice asked.

"Actually," Christy said. "I haven't made a decision. Or rather I should say that I had not made a decision. But now I have."

Neil shook his head. "Yes, I suppose the train derailing must look very much like a message from above that you are not to return to Cutter Gap."

"What nonsense, Neil," Miss Alice said. "As though God goes around derailing trains. I rather suspect we'll find there was a small rock slide. Really!"

"Don't keep us in suspense," David said.

"I have decided to follow my heart and return to Cutter Gap," Christy said.

The doctor and David both brightened amazingly. Lance looked crestfallen.

"But what about the chance to be with your family again?" Lance asked. "What about your home?"

"Just before the wreck, I was thinking of Cutter Gap," Christy said. "And I realized, to my surprise, that when I thought of it, I thought of it as home. Cutter Gap is my home now, as much as Asheville. And David and Neil and Ruby Mae and Miss Alice and all my students—they're also my family now, along with my parents and friends in Asheville. I guess what's happened is that I have two homes. And a larger family than I'd realized."

"Well, what will we ever do for a teacher?" Mr. Barclay asked. "Who else can we find with your unique experience?"

"You do realize, Christy, that the Cutter Gap mission may not even survive without funds," David pointed out.

"I've been thinking about that," Christy said. "I wonder, Mr. Barclay . . . I have very little to teach anyone about teaching itself—"

"Nonsense," Mr. Barclay protested.

"But between myself and Miss Alice and David, I dare say we could manage to train some bright, willing teacher. Perhaps if the teacher you find could spend a couple of months with us . . ."

"You would do that?" Mr. Barclay said. "You would train our teacher for us?"

"Yes, she would," the doctor said suddenly. "And in exchange, you could help support the Cutter Gap mission."

"Doctor!" Miss Alice protested. "We give our help freely. We do not charge for our services."

Mr. Barclay laughed. "The doctor is a very direct man, Miss Alice. And he's right. I think we can help each other out. Two successful missions are surely better than one. And the people of the mountains need a mission as much as those in the city."

"Yes," Lance agreed. "After all, many of our poor and ignorant are mountain men, only recently come to the city."

Mr. Barclay nodded. "And so are some of our richer and more successful people. In fact, Lance, since we are so near to Cutter Gap, I believe it may be time for you to meet someone very important in our family."

"A member of our family? Here?" Lance looked around skeptically at the mountains.

"My great aunt, your great-grand aunt," Mr. Barclay told his son. "Her name is Isabelle. Although I believe people just call her Granny. Granny Barclay."

"Aha! Then you are related to Granny!" the doctor cried. "I believe I distinctly heard your wife deny any such thing."

"Well, Mrs. Barclay is very concerned about what society might think. But as for me, I'll always be the grandson of a mountain man. And I'm proud of it."

"Well, then," Christy said, "we'd better be going. I have lesson plans to prepare, and I miss my home."

"Even the hogs?" Neil and David and Miss Alice asked at exactly the same moment.

Christy grinned. "Well, maybe not the hogs."

About Catherine Marshall

Catherine Marshall LeSourd (1914–1983), a *New York Times* bestselling author, is best known for her novel *Christy*. Based on the life of her mother, a teacher of mountain children in poverty-stricken Tennessee, *Christy* captured the hearts of millions and became a popular CBS television series. As her mother reminisced around the kitchen table at Evergreen Farm, Catherine probed for details and insights into the rugged lives of these Appalachian highlanders.

The Christy® of Cutter Gap series, based on the characters of the beloved novel, contains expanded adventures filled with romance, excitement, and intrigue.

Catherine also wrote *Julie*, a sweeping novel of love and adventure, courage and commitment, tragedy and triumph, in a Pennsylvania steel town during the Great Depression.

Catherine's first husband, Peter Marshall, was Chaplain of the U.S. Senate, and her intimate biography of him, *A Man Called Peter*, became an international bestseller and Academy Award Nominated movie. The story shares the power of this dynamic man's love for his God and for the woman he married.

A beloved inspirational writer and speaker, Catherine's enduring career spanned four decades and six continents, and reached over 30 million readers.

CHRISTY'S ADVENTURES CONTINUE IN...

When Ruby Mae, Bessie, and Clara discover gold in Dead Man's Creek, they form an exclusive group calling themselves "The Princess Club." Soon everyone in Cutter Gap is racing to find more gold.

Christy watches in dismay as the girls, and soon the whole town, are torn apart by greed and envy. Can she find a way to heal the bitter divisions caused by a handful of gold?

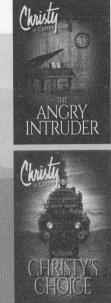